GOLD MAN REVIEW

ISSUE 11

Gold Man Review is published annually by Gold Man Publishing.

The editors invite submissions of previously unpublished works of fiction, nonfiction, and poetry. Manuscripts can be submitted at www.goldmanpublishing.com by following our submission guidelines.

Address all requests to:
Heather Cuthbertson
Editor-in-Chief
Heather.Cuthbertson@GoldManPublishing.com

Contents

Issue 11 Editor's Letter

Let's talk about the elephant in the room: Covid. It's hard not to see life these days in a pre and post Covid mindset. It's amazing how much I miss the little things. At first, I'll admit, I wasn't sad to see some of them go, such as the endless parties at Chuck E.Cheese, being my kids' soccer coach, and the Jog-a-Thon. The Jog-a-Thon is an event that my kids' school does at the start of fall. Every time I saw that dreaded manila envelope come home with all those lines for "pledges," I'd cringe. What was I supposed to do? Hit up my neighbors, whose kids also went to the same school, and ask them to donate money to my children's athletic prowess when they themselves were scrambling to do the same? I did what most parents probably did and shoved some money in the envelope and called it a day. On the morning of the Jog-A-Thon, I'd throw on my leggings and run the makeshift track in the field, partitioned off with orange cones. I hate running. I'd rather get a root canal. I'd rather do burpees and, trust me, that's saying something. While the rest of the parents shot each other forced smiles with every lap and Dixie cup of water downed, there was always that one mom or dad who ran like the turf was cotton and outpaced their kid by a quarter of a lap while shouting encouraging montages. The Jog-a-Thon ended with popsicles and pictures and the thought of having a full year before I had to do it again. Until it didn't. It stopped. At first, I was happy. "Thank you, Covid. No Jog-A-Thon." But now I miss the hell out of it. This year the kids did the Jog-A-Thon, but no parents were allowed to participate and for the first time, I wanted to. I wanted to run that makeshift track, sipping water out of Dixie cups, and hanging out with my kids. It was my son's first time doing it and I wasn't there. I know there's so much more to life than the Jog-A-Thon, but at the same time it's those little things that make life. We've all missed out on something. The Jog-a-thon is small. I know that. Some of us have had to miss people and people should be at the center of everything.

We're in a great divide. Sides have been taken and the proverbial line in the sand has been drawn. I don't think there's ever been a time when division has done us any good. We all have an opinion of how things should be, what decisions we should make as a collective, and the right path we should take. But all these opinions have only led to less discussion and more arguing, more bitterness and hate. The things I've seen others post on social media has shocked me. People wishing the worst on others and saying it with such flippancy that I wonder what sort of humanity is left within them. What world do we live in that this is okay? I'm not an outwardly vocal person, but I have opinions like everyone else and I'll admit, sometimes those opinions have been without merit. The circumstances that changed my mind didn't come from others belittlement and venom, but from a place of love and care. We're all capable of changing our minds because, at the end of the day, the heart knows what's true. My mother told me that people might not always remember the things you've said or done, but they'll never forget how you made them feel. One day this is going to be over and that will be all that's left: how we made others feel and that's what I try to remember.

As this year draws to a close and 2022 is fast approaching, let's stop focusing on "out there" and instead on what we can do from the corner of the world fate has delivered us. For me, that's Gold Man Review. Once a year, I get to deliver good news to the contributors who are selected for publication and do my best to present their work the best way I can. That's what I'm doing from my spot on the planet but we each have something to offer that can make things better. Make someone laugh. Share more jokes on social media. What happened to those food pics? I'd like more of those. We need more of all of it because good things and bad things are happening all the time. It was happening before Covid and will continue to do so long after we've moved on from this virus. After losing both my parents within months of each other, experience has taught me that when tragedy comes, it's unannounced, quick, and leaves you grappling long after its gone. It's deeply personal and horribly painful. So many people right now are dealing with tragedy and showing a bit of kindness really goes a long way. For those that are hurting, let's focus on spreading more grace and goodwill, instead of division. Let's do it for them. And above all, when you see someone wishing death on another on social media, block that person.

Here's to a better 2022.

Heather Cuthbertson
Editor-in-Chief
Gold Man Review

Gold Man Review Editors
Issue 11

Heather Cuthbertson
Editor-in-Chief

Nicklas Roetto
Project Editor

Daniel Link
Editor

Ashley Rich
Editor

2021 Gold Man Review Readers
Nancy Bennett
Geri Copitch
Alex Von Dachenhausen

From the Treetops

seth jani

No last edges here.
The wilderness keeps unfolding
its purple temples, and far
as the eye can see
the guttural blade of darkness
cuts new roads.
So much fear is tied
to our belief
in terminal endings,
but the knot is always loosening
into something that doesn't resemble
a knot. We're all tied up in the world.
It keeps going,
stretched with grief and sunlight,
with the small shadows
of yesterday's birds.
We turn to our better angels
and find our lives are populous.
Presences flecked like bits of gold
through every broken river.
You're not alone, O precious one,
the wind conducts
an armada of voices.

fiction

Dog Story
l.l. babb

My wife, Francine, had been dead six months when I ran into Billy Wilson at the grocery store, and he mentioned under his breath that there was a cull going on that night. It all came back to me at once—the musty scent of fur, the feel of warm, writhing muscles under my hands. Billy offered to pick me up that evening and drive me out there for a look. Just a look, I told myself. His souped-up Mustang was a lot faster than my old pickup if the authorities got wind of the cull and we had to make a quick getaway. Even though it had been twenty-five years since my last infraction, I couldn't quite shake the sense that the cops were still watching, waiting for me to slip up again. After the last incident, I had promised Francine I was done with that life, done with the hiding and sneaking around. But now she was gone, and I knew what I did didn't matter to anyone. Not anymore.

Billy cut the lights on the Mustang roughly half a mile before we turned onto a narrow dirt road off Old Westside. An occasional ring of redwoods rose like skyscrapers next to us as we drove deeper into the forest. Bay trees and Scotch broom closed in and brushed the sides of the car, making Billy wince. But he was into the dogs as much as I was, and little things like scratches on his precious Mustang weren't going to stop us. Billy was young and single, more boy than man even though he was in his mid-forties. He wiped at his nose with the back of his hand when he told me his boxer mix had passed the summer before. That dog had been a real beast, solid as a tank with teeth like a shark. Incredibly gentle despite its size and those terrible teeth. Sweet, affectionate, goofy, and illegal as hell.

As soon as we drew close to the river, I could hear the dogs through the open car window, whining and yipping. The sound made something tighten in my chest, a vise squeezing my lungs, and I leaned forward in my seat. I hadn't touched a real dog in years. My fingers gripped then released my knees over and over like I already had an animal in my hands.

Francine had owned a dog before the cancer came. Or what passes for a dog nowadays. A "designer dog" bred without vocal cords, hypoallergenic, non-shedding, flea and tick resistant. Predisposed to bond with whoever fed it. Poop that looked like a purple lozenge of lavender soap and smelled like it too. No canine teeth at all and the rest of the bite so dull it couldn't make a mark in warm butter. The dog had the personality of a Roomba. I couldn't see the point, but Francine loved that thing. Queenie. What Queenie did best was follow Francine from room to room. She slept most of the time. Or sat staring at the wall. They'd bred any leg strength out of the dog, so she couldn't run more than a couple of yards without tiring. Bred out the instinct to run even if she had been able. As far as I was concerned, that was not a dog.

A cull was never in the same place more than once. Tonight's was on a wide sandbar on the bank of the river. On the other side of the water, I could make out in the icy moonlight the neat rows at the back of a vineyard, the bare canes reaching up into the sky like gnarled fingers. In a few months the vines would leaf out and muffle any sound, but now I worried that the dogs' whining would carry across the vineyard to where someone might be sleeping. I didn't recognize any of the men down with the dogs. I hoped they knew what they were doing. I couldn't imagine calling my son, Mr. CPA, from jail asking for bail money.

Half a dozen cars and trucks were parked on the dirt road, a few with their headlights shining down at the cull. There were probably thirty dogs down there, all skinny, short-haired, and skittish. Stray dogs, mutts picked up from the backstreets of Ensenada or Tijuana and smuggled across the border. Some sat scratching at their ears; others cowered with their tails between their legs, the whites of their eyes showing. All of them were beautiful, all of them were the real things, and I knew right then I had made a mistake in coming.

Billy and I got out of the car and walked down to the cull. The men were all dressed the same—jeans, baseball caps pulled down low, cowboy boots, hands deep in jacket pockets against the cold. My kind of people. Billy said hi to someone he recognized—a burly guy who had brought his son, about twelve years old, I guessed, sticking close to his dad. I marveled at the insanity of bringing a child to a cull, but on the other hand, you had to admire a father for wanting to introduce his son to genuine dogs.

Most of the dogs were Chihuahua mixes—walleyed and snaggletoothed. Easy to hide but almost impossible to keep quiet. You didn't want a noisy dog unless you lived far out in the country. There were a couple of dogs that looked like they had some kind of heeler in them, way back in their lineage. None of the dogs were over thirty pounds. The sellers seemed knowledgeable enough to avoid anything that involved the breeds that carried real jailtime—no Akitas, Dobermans, Rottweilers, or shepherd mixes. You could get ten years for possession of one of those. Possession of a pit bull or even a pit bull mix resulted in a mandatory sentence of twenty years or more even if there was only a drop of pit DNA in the dog.

I squatted down and let the dogs come sniff me. A couple of the bolder Chihuahua mixes trotted over, wiggling like mad when I petted them. I had some chunks of cheese in my jacket pocket, and as I handed them out, more dogs came to me. It had been so long since I had touched a dog that I almost grabbed one of the little guys and held him to my face to inhale him. I let them lick my fingers and put their paws on my knee and stare up at me with their googly eyes. Some of the dogs limped over and shied away when I offered my hand to them as if they thought the cheese was a trick, that I might hurt them. They were all malnourished—ribs showing through their fur, their coats matted and dull. Beaten probably. Kicked, starved, and unloved. I wanted to take them all.

A larger dog approached. She probably weighed about twenty pounds—way too thin for how tall she was. She had a fawn-colored face with dark fur around her eyes like kohl, a black cleft of hair down the middle of her forehead, and tilted eyebrows that made her look worried. She was trailing a puppy behind her, and I could see her teats were still swollen though the pup looked healthy and old enough to be weaned. She walked toward me leading with her nose and sniffing at me from several feet away. I held out the cheese and she inched closer, nudging the puppy to make sure it stayed behind. When she finally reached my hand, she took the piece of cheese delicately, then rested the tip of her muzzle on the ends of my fingers and gazed up into my eyes. I had the same sensation I'd experienced when I first met Francine all those years ago, that feeling of finding something I had needed but never realized I lacked. That sense of "Oh, *there* she is."

There was no way I could take the dog and her puppy. I was on the far side of my sixties. My house was tiny, my yard a thirty-by-thirty-foot square. I had neighbors on three sides—good, friendly people, but how willing would they be to ignore not one but two illegal dogs right under their noses? Plus, you never knew how big a puppy might get. When the U.S. started outlawing the breeds, big dogs were the first to go, dumped down in Mexico to fend for themselves. The puppy looked fluffy and sweet and small, but there was no way of telling what breed it was, what genes ran through its blood. You never knew what to expect when you got a puppy. It could turn into a ninety-pound liability.

One of the sellers squatted down beside me and scratched the bitch's ears. "This one is a real sweetheart," he said. "She won't give you any trouble. Good dog." The dog turned and looked at the man.

I stood and perused the rest of the cull. Billy had scooped up some godawful little pug/poodle/Chihuahua/beagle/Heinz 57 mix that nestled under his chin. The dog couldn't have weighed more than four pounds. Billy's eyes were full of tears. I looked away so as not to embarrass him, but I knew how he felt. Big grown men blubbering about the dogs we couldn't live without. That was us. That was all of us down in the cull.

The twelve-year-old took the puppy. I realized that this was one more reason why you didn't bring a little kid to a cull. There was no reasoning with them once they found a kindred spirit, a fellow child. I never would've taken Daniel to a cull, at any age. Francine put her foot down about owning an illegal dog when we adopted Daniel. We had to be upstanding citizens and set a good example and all that. Besides, I could just see the prissy way Daniel would have waded among the animals, hands held up high so nothing could touch him, his face screwed up in fear and distaste. My kid was not a dog person.

The seller who had spoken to me held onto the bitch's collar, her worried eyes trained on the boy as he walked away with her puppy. Her whole life must have been one loss after another.

On the way home, Billy wouldn't put his mutt down. He drove us back to town one-handed, the little dog still glued to his neck. My dog sat in the backseat staring straight ahead, concentrating on her future as if it was being revealed to her through the windshield. Next to her were two sacks of Mexican kibble to help with the transition to whatever home-cooked food we would be serving up in the future. There was no going to the grocery store for dog food—designer dogs ate soy and kale pellets laced with chemicals to make their feces smell good.

"What are you going to name that godawful thing?" I asked Billy.

He gave me a side-eyed glare. "Haven't decided yet."

"It's so ugly, it's kind of cute," I said, as a sort of apology. Then after he didn't say anything, I added, "It's a fine dog," and he grunted. Apology accepted.

It was after midnight when Billy dropped me off in front of my house. The dog relieved herself on the front lawn, and I brought her in. Her nails clicked on the hardwood floors as she went from room to room, checking out her surroundings. I got her a bowl of water and went outside to hose down the lawn where she had peed. I was no novice—telltale, circular brown spots on your lawn were a red flag. So were piles of dog poop left anywhere or even disposed of in the trash. Everything had to be cleaned up immediately and flushed down the toilet. Owning a real dog was a challenge, but for people like Billy and me, it was well worth it.

The answering machine on my landline was blinking. Four missed calls. All the messages were from my daughter-in-law, sounding increasingly panicked that I wasn't answering the phone. It was too late to call back. I could only hope that she hadn't alerted the cavalry, that I wouldn't find a couple of social workers knocking on my door first thing in the morning for a senior wellness check. Jennifer was from one of those big, close-knit families who were all in each other's business constantly. Very touchy-feely, always checking in with each other, how's everyone doing? She didn't understand Daniel and I weren't that kind of family.

I grabbed an old blanket from the linen closet and arranged it next to the bed. The dog circled and circled for a minute before lying down and resting her head on her front paws. "You need a name," I said. A million years ago, before we decided to go the adoption route, Francine had been pregnant for seventeen whole weeks. We had this prenatal guidebook, and every week Francine would check the size of the baby according to the book. Garbanzo bean, lima bean, walnut, turnip. We lost our little girl at turnip. We hadn't even decided on a name yet. She was just our little turnip when we spoke about the baby after the miscarriage.

Francine had named Queenie. This time the naming would be all up to me. I wondered what I had done getting a dog, an illegal dog, alone, at my age. Maybe my mind was starting to go. How would I know? Who would notice?

I woke in the morning with the sense I was being watched. Sometime in the night the dog had crawled up onto the bed, her head on Francine's pillow. Her eyes stared into mine, unflinching. Those dark, tilted eyebrows were more pronounced in the daylight. I couldn't help feeling that the dog had me pegged and was judging this new, though not unheard of, lapse in my character. "Francine?" I said, feeling immediately ridiculous. Francine had been a rule follower. There was no way she would come back as my illegal dog.

The dog stood and stretched and waited until I was out of bed before she jumped down to the floor. She scratched at the back door and I let her out, reasonably sure that none of my neighbors would notice her at this time of day. She careened out, came up short at the fence, then slowly circled the yard, checking out the situation. I made myself a cup of instant coffee and called my daughter-in-law.

"Dad," she said. "We were getting so worried. Where were you?"

I flinched at being called Dad. I always did. What was it with people pretending you were instant family just because you were thrown together?

"Here and there," I said, putting a lot of jolly in my voice. "Out with a friend."

"Well, Danny and I want to invite you over for dinner tonight."

Another flinch. Danny. Jennifer was the only one ever to call my kid that. He was Daniel when we adopted him—six years old, reed thin, already a serious old man, black-framed glasses too big for his face. He told us he liked to be called Daniel, not Danny, not Dan. Standoffish kid, awkward as all get-out. It had been love at first sight for Francine. Me, not so much. Daniel and I never really warmed to each other.

Outside, the dog was pacing by the fence, her head up as if she had seen a squirrel walking across the rail. The fence was a good six feet tall, redwood planks, pressurized wood posts set in concrete. I'd made it myself when we first moved in. Sturdy as the trees it came from.

"Tonight's no good," I said. "I've got stuff to take care of."

"But we haven't seen you in months," Jennifer said. "It's not good for you to be alone so much."

"Another time then," I said. "I'll let you know."

After I hung up, I called the dog back into the house. She came reluctantly, stopping several times to look back over her shoulder.

She stood and tolerated me as I rubbed her ears and massaged her shoulders and back.

"We definitely need to get you a name," I said. I had always been keen on giving my dogs people names. None of this Rover or Fido stuff for me. I scrambled an egg and added it to some kibble in a china bowl. "How about Linda? Or Paula?"

The dog sniffed at the food, then trotted into the living room to stare out the sliding glass door into the backyard.

What can I say about the week that followed? She wouldn't eat. She accepted my petting stoically. She stared out into the back garden. She never wagged her tail, but when I woke each morning, she was there on Francine's pillow, staring at me with those hopeful, unblinking eyes. As each day progressed, a weight seemed to fall upon her, heavier and heavier, until by nightfall she could barely lift her head to look at me. I figured it was only a matter of time before she knew how good her life could be. I was patient. I could wait. She was a good dog—no barking, no chewing, no signs of any aggressive behavior, housebroken to a fault. I fussed about in the kitchen trying to find something she would eat. She wasn't tempted by anything I offered—chicken, liver, steak, bacon. I gave her a bath, wrapped her in a towel, and built a fire in the fireplace to warm her. I told her about Francine and how much they would have liked each other (a bit of a stretch, I know, but nobody was going to call me out on it). I read her the newspaper, discussed the current political situation, let her sit on the couch while we watched television. I couldn't settle on a name for her. I'd call her something for a couple of hours, then change it to something else. Nothing felt right.

Saturday morning my daughter-in-law called again.

"I'm not taking no for an answer," Jennifer said. "If you don't come here tonight, we're loading everything up and bringing dinner to you."

I sipped at my coffee. The dog was in the backyard, circling the fence. The circling round and round had become her habit whenever she was outside, head up, looking for something. There had been a hard frost the night before, and the grass was tipped in white. She had lost weight in the week I had her. Her face looked gaunt.

"Can you come around five?" Jennifer said. "Or earlier?" I felt that familiar irritation at being forced into doing something I didn't want to do or feeling something that I didn't want to feel. Who were these people to me anyway?

"Now look…" I began, just as I saw the dog use the corner of the fence, where it met at a right angle, to scrabble up like a monkey and disappear over the top into the front yard.

"Shit!" I spit my mouthful of coffee back into the cup. "I gotta go," I said, hanging up the phone. I was wearing my bathrobe and a pair of boxers, my skinny legs and knobby knees not something I was prepared to show the world. I raced back to my bedroom and threw on the clothes I'd left on the floor the night before. I was out the door in less than a minute. I scanned the street to see which direction the dog might have run, but she was nowhere in sight.

My next-door neighbor, Phil, was out on his lawn picking up his paper. "Hey, Tom," he said, waving at me. "What a morning, right?" What did that mean? Had he seen something? Or was he just referring to the cold? Phil was even older than I was. His eyes behind the monstrous lenses of his glasses appeared dark and beady as if viewed from the wrong end of a telescope. If he had seen something dart past him, would he even recognize it as a dog? I couldn't read his expression and I couldn't ask.

I dug into my pants pocket for the truck keys. They weren't there. I ran back into the house. They weren't in the bowl by the door or on the kitchen table. Why did I never put them where they belonged? I tore up the bedroom, throwing the covers off the bed. I finally found them in the pocket of a jacket that was hanging over a chair in the dining room. At least twenty minutes had passed since the dog disappeared. I had to find her before the cops did. She'd be euthanized for sure. There would be no way to help her.

I sat in my truck for a moment trying to think. I felt that same kind of helplessness I had when Francine died. Then it came to me. I knew where she was.

The dog was there of course, down on the sandbar. She had a good head start, and it took me several passes to find the opening in the woods to that dirt road, but even so the place along the river where the cull had taken place had to be a good four or five miles from my house. She must have run at top speed all the way there. She was lying on her side near the water, panting heavily. She didn't raise her head when she saw me making my way down the embankment, just flicked her eyes in my direction and then looked away.

I sat down next to her and put my hand on her side. Her fur was frigid. I could feel her heart hammering against her rib cage. The pads of her feet were torn and bleeding. I picked her up like a baby, carried her up the embankment, and put her in the cab of the truck. Then I drove to Billy Wilson's house.

When I knocked on his door, I heard a sharp yip, then the sound of footsteps and doors slamming shut inside. I probably should have called. After a few minutes the door opened a crack to reveal a fraction of Billy's wary face. When he saw who it was, he motioned me inside. Back when I used to keep illegal dogs, some of my fellow conspirators had "safe rooms," a place where they could stash their dog and nobody could hear it. Francine never allowed me to do anything like that at our house, but I'd seen a lot of them. Laundry rooms lined with thick felt padding, egg cartons thumbtacked to the walls, moving blankets hung like curtains. Billy, I knew, had an entire bedroom tricked out for his dog, complete with a hidden door behind a bookshelf. He lived alone; he had no one to answer to. His safe room wasn't doing much good this morning to muffle the sound of his new mutt. I could hear its humanlike shrieking from where we stood in the foyer.

"That's the pug in her. Hold on a sec," he said. He retrieved the dog and I followed him into the kitchen. "She'll get used to the room at some point." Billy kissed the dog between her ears. I watched the trusting way the dog turned her head to look up at him and I felt a wrench of jealousy. "This is Gracie," Billy said, "you know, like George Burns and Gracie Allen? She's decided she's the comedian and I'm her straight man."

"That's a great name for her," I said to Billy. "A perfect name."

I got the address of the guy at the cull, the guy Billy knew with the kid who took my dog's puppy. My dog—I couldn't really call her that. She wasn't my dog. She wasn't ever going to be my dog, I could see that now.

The guy and his kid lived a few hours out in the country on one of those dusty, rundown ranches in the foothills. A donkey behind a falling-down fence, a half-dozen chickens running around in the muddy driveway. A fallow garden plot overseen by a scarecrow made out of a hazmat suit stuffed with newspaper. Mom coming out of the house with an apron on. A life I might have imagined for myself at one time.

Thank god for that kid. He could instantly see that my dog and her pup had to be together. It took some time and convincing from both of us for his parents to come around—time and money and some vague promises that there would be more money coming if needed. I knew I'd done the right thing when the dogs saw each other as I lifted mine from the truck. If dogs had arms they would have held on to each other and never let go, the way Francine and Daniel used to hug each time they saw each other after being apart for a while. And here I was again, on the outside looking in.

"She needs a name," I told the kid as I was climbing back into my truck. "What do you think you're going to call her?"

The kid turned to look at her. She was running in dizzy circles around her puppy like a crazed animal, delirious with happiness despite her torn feet and utter exhaustion.

"Donut," the kid said.

"That's a great name," I said. "That's perfect."

"Keep in touch," the father said tersely, but I could tell he was a man who would do anything for his son. The dog would be fine here. I watched the little ranch recede in my rearview mirror, and when I turned to get on the two-lane highway, it was as if a door slammed shut behind me, another part of my life gone forever. One loss after another.

I didn't get back home until late afternoon. Daniel's car was in the driveway with its doors hanging open. I could see the back of Daniel's head in the driver's seat and Jennifer's legs sticking out the passenger side. Jennifer leaped out of the car as I pulled the truck up to the curb.

"Oh my god," she said, barreling toward me. "We thought something awful had happened. You hung up the phone like the house was on fire."

Daniel got wearily out of the car.

In that moment, I saw the dogs at the cull, the ones bounding over to me, wiggling with excitement and wagging their tails, the ones hanging back. The ones you could tell had been loved by a human at some point; the ones who knew loss and rejection. Jennifer's coattails flapping behind her as she ran; Daniel's tired face looking at me warily. Daniel. He stayed by the car, curled his fingers to study his nails, and adjusted his glasses, studiously nonchalant, guarded. He was the same little boy from all those years ago, still expecting the emotional blow that was sure to come. I might not have created this adult, but I was guilty of contributing to who he became. It suddenly felt like I had squandered something tangible away, could almost feel the watery way it had slipped through my fingers, and I would never be able to claw it back.

Then Jennifer was on me, hugging me, patting my back, squeezing my arms. She was a tiny hummingbird of a woman, quick and blurry, her hands moving over me as if searching for broken bones.

"I'm fine," I said. "Just went for a drive."

"We were about to call the police," Jennifer said. "Weren't we, Danny?"

Daniel ducked his head, seeming embarrassed. "Not really."

Francine always said I liked dogs more than people. This was mostly true. People were complicated. They took more effort, more time, more patience. Francine also said that loving someone else's kid wasn't exactly the same as loving your own, maybe not at first, but you could definitely get there. That took patience too.

"I'm sorry, son," I said, walking up to him. "I'm really, truly sorry. For everything." I wanted to say more, but my throat closed up over the words like it was sealing off a terrible abyss. Any more might undo me. It was the best I could do for now.

fiction

Cherry Blossom Ending

jennifer kim

I always marveled at the fact that there was a cherry tree in our neighborhood. I would say "front yard," but nobody had a front yard in this concrete town of cheap, last-minute cement.

Everything here dries, burns to a crisp under the harsh, unforgiving gaze of California sunlight. The cement sidewalks might as well be all oceans combined, because all it does is suck up heat, heat, heat.

You make a pact with your neighbor–I get to tie my string to the end of your house to hang my laundry, and you get to tie *your* string to the end of *my* house and–yeah, all right, go fuck yourself, hang yourself, go die, you worthless piece of shit.

I still remember the day that I learned laundry's not the only thing to hang. And the sun takes no prisoners—even souls can dry up when laid bare across cement in California.

But then, there was that cherry tree. Its soft-colored petals, promising some tinge of pink that you could only otherwise find caught on the fringe of a cotton candy cloud three minutes before sunrise, were the only breath of something translucent, something bearable, here.

The day she died, cherry blossoms scattered all over the sky, borne by a cold wind.

You told me, "Autumn is coming, if it's not upon us already."

My eyes traced the whispering petals spiraling in the air and disappearing fast over the concrete, but sight cannot keep beautiful things where they are, and memory is faulty. I asked you, "Where do they all go?"

And you said, "Don't cry," already knowing that my soft heart had gone straight to mourning for all the things we cannot keep.

Pure Luxury

nellie papsdorf

I am angry that you are dead and other people famous.

Dusty. Ashed. Three quarters and a used can and a coffee
in the cupholder as we drive to the coast you'll never see again.

You also had a crooked kid's teeth. A softer snarl
in an adult mouth. Co-smoking, co-corn dogs,

co-judging the car that plaits without warning. The smell
of soap on your fingers after a smoke. I can't shake

the taste of sour cotton. What I'd do
for a soft tut and a wink. I wish I could show you

this sexy crevice at the ocean. The splintered rocks
where the water spits back and gargles.

A putrid foam that lingers after the snowcapped locks.

Killing Todd

james giffin

Todd must die.

I'll tell you about Todd. He lives two floors above me in the residential hotel I've just moved into. He's on the fourth floor, so to get there, you have to ride the funky-smelling elevator or exhaust yourself climbing the trashed staircase. My unit is on the second floor, where streams of cockroaches are more likely to appear flowing out of the garbage chute and skittering up the hallway.

You'd be amazed by this building, by this neighborhood. Until the shooting downstairs on Turk before they cleaned everything up, the sidewalk was constantly blocked by a cloud of crack-possessed zombies—weathered, ashen, and toothless; scanning the ground, bent over, and twirly-eyed; guarding flames from the breeze. These are the streets that parents drive their snotty teens through so they realize how cushy they have it back in suburbia. They call this the Tenderloin, and I've already been living around here off-and-on for several years; the TL felt like home long before I gained a roof at the Dalt. Options for new friends in the building seem limited—most residents are seniors, shut-ins, developmentally disabled, criminal, or even violent, and often live in filth.

Todd's not a senior. He looks like he's in his early thirties—slightly older than me—and he keeps his unit relatively clean. By my first impression, he seems no more mentally ill than I am. The only crime of his I'm aware of is his use of crystal meth. I don't judge; I'm not some cuddly, innocent cutie. Considering the lack of roaches freely skittering up and down his unit's walls, his age, and perceived mental acuity, his drug use hardly bothers me at all. Todd also happens to be awake at the same odd hours that I am, and he's non-judgmental when I look like I do at three or four a.m., when my bed covers have turned into fire out of drought and have pushed me, itching for company and a free hit of speed, to the keypad of my phone.

"Honey, you're better than that," says my friend Brahim. I've known Brahim for years. He was a resident of the Dalt Hotel, too, until moving out shortly after I moved in. He knows the building and he knows what people think of each other in the building. He grimaces as he exhales smoke from his American Spirit and says, "Look at him and then, look at *you.*" Brahim explains that as individuals, we are judged by the company we keep. Even though I already know this is true, I hate it and wish it wasn't so. There seems to be another reason that Brahim wants to steer me away from Todd, but when I press him, his answers are vague. "Girl, trust me," he says, "don't hang around him."

I bring the discussion to one of the few friendly women who live in the building. "Who, Todd?" Felicity asks as I pass her a freshly-lit joint. I'm sitting on the ground in her unit and she's sitting on her bed. "Oh," she says, frowning, "he's a tweaker." Her tone is even, as if she needn't explain what this fact means for one's reputation. "He was here before I moved in. People say he used to be normal." She takes a few puffs from the joint, holding the smoke, and hands it back to me. "He's nice and all," she says after exhaling, "but I don't fuck with people like that."

Todd wears the same pair of Guess jeans every day, which hang stiffly about his boyish legs that absolutely refuse to gain weight. He wears tee shirts too tight, even by gay guy standards. Only rarely does he wear anything over them (presumably because he's always inside); if he does, it's a generic grey hoodie. He has short hair that was once dirty blond, but without sun and the vital nutrients most of us find in food, Todd's hair has turned mouse brown. It's undernourished and lackluster, and probably feels like something between hay and the wire bristles of a scrub brush. His complexion is light, the veins nearly visible beneath his skin, and dark circles have permanently formed around his eyes like a raccoon.

Todd has a poor pooch named Zippy, some sort of puffball terrier that does everything within its canine ability to cling to my shin and scream *Help!* whenever it sees me. The animal only seems lifted from its depressed state of learned helplessness after its monthly bath, or when Todd remembers to feed it. When Todd has gathered sufficient remorse from his harsh words after a one-way row, he makes up with his pet by violently combing its fur with his fingers. "Daddy didn't mean it," he says, "you're my little dancing queen," and he puppeteers Zippy's paws to the beat of ABBA. The relationship is textbook trans-species codependency, and it, at times, puts my morality to the test deciding if I should take a stand by anonymously alerting the SPCA.

Todd is insistent. He is eager for friendship, which lets off a noxious cloud of vulnerability (do I let off a noxious cloud, too?). If he hasn't seen me around, if I've been hibernating, or any other time when I least want to have Todd show up at my front door is when he comes knocking. He wakes me from thick, dream-heavy sleep—my cellphone usually reports a range of ten p.m. to one a.m.—saying, "It's Todd," loudly and repeatedly. "I haven't seen you around for a few days," he says. "I was worried." After bribing me to hang out upstairs, and with increasing use of his pipe, he begins to whine to himself, back and forth, or mutter little strings of nothing, leaving no room for me in the conversation. The more cranked he gets, the more he paces the length of his room, jabbing his heels into the floor and flapping about wildly, as if he loathes his own limbs and is trying to ditch them from the rest of his body. He puts on a DVD and turns up the volume, already stuck with his hand in his pants. I'm worried about people hearing all the nasty grunting sounds through the open window. I have to come up with an excuse to get out of here, which is hard to do in the middle of the night since nothing else is happening. When I get up to quietly leave, he's luckily too fixated on the TV to notice his door close behind me.

Unlike me, Todd doesn't drink alcohol. Instead, he buys two-liter bottles of soda which almost always end up toppled over on the thin carpet. It's happened so many times that whenever I walk out into the hallway after standing in his room, my shoes will smack and stick to the linoleum from the tacky sugar.

Todd and I were first introduced in this very building about a year ago. We played around for a few hours, though, in my defense, I was horny over the rainbow on Delsym and meth. This was back when Todd was more "normal," with fleeting signs of attractiveness (my standards aren't terribly high, but that's another story—or is it?). I hadn't seen Todd again until moving in just recently, and while I do recognize the man I once found attractive, I could never again be with him sexually. Maybe my standards are higher now because the idea of his skin on mine is repulsive. Brahim told me that Todd was once arrested and had to go to jail for two or so weeks, and when he came back detoxed and clean, it was like he was a different person. His voice was deeper, slower, and he was calmer, less hyperactive. But when he got back to using again, his voice rose and he started to skitter about, never holding still.

The exchange between Todd and me left a nasty taste in my mouth, and not just because of the cough syrup. It happened almost a year before we would end up sharing the same address. San Francisco is a small city, made smaller if you're a gay man in it, and you learn to shake off the awkwardness when running into previous hook-ups. I thought Todd was doing just as good a job as me at not clinging to this incident in our past, until I notice him uttering some strange comments when we are in private.

"I don't expect anything in return," he says after bumming me a Marlboro Red 100. "We're just seeing where this goes."

Well, *I'm* not seeing. I know. It's not going any goddamn place. I'm simply seeing how far the freebies last until he asks me to pitch in, like a normal person would. If he was a friend, I would've offered something as soon as I had it in my pocket.

I start rationalizing that I don't really need to be smoking. Don't need to be digging for change or bothering Todd for cigarettes at all. I have these old nicotine patches a doctor once prescribed me somewhere in my apartment. They are in three different sizes; you start with the biggest (Step One) and taper off with the smallest (Step Three). I keep telling myself that I'll start using them to quit when I'm ready.

Whenever I'm feeling stuck in life, I ask my friend Sasha for advice. She's to-the-point and blunt, so I know I'll get a straight response. After relating the background story to her, I say, "So, what do you think? You've met him. How do I kill this guy off without hurting his feelings?"

"You can't," Sasha says and blows out a plume of smoke. "If you want him to stop talking to you—and I think it's best for a few reasons—just completely ignore him. Every woman who's dated anyone knows this. The way to break it off is *to* hurt his feelings."

"The last week or so, I've been trying to ignore him. I ignore his calls and text messages. I hole myself up in my room for days until he comes banging on my door and I'm lying there silent feeling like Anne fucking Frank." I realize I'm getting worked up, so I slow my breathing down and try to relax. "Then he'll catch me in the lobby the minute I run outside. It's miserable," I say and put my face in my hands.

"So you caved?" She takes a drag from her Camel Crush, shaking her head. "Try harder next time, baby."

I'll tell you why Todd must die. Todd is the softness inside me that's become toxic. He represents every uneven, unfair relationship in my life (of which there have been a handful). It's hard for me to say no to people—I suppose I'm the "nice" guy, the overly compassionate one—and this has left me vulnerable to manipulation. The toxicity feeds on the niceness, on the inability to say no. This all happens despite the fact I'm perceptive enough to see it. As an avoider of confrontation, sometimes I believe things will work out if I just stay quiet.

I consider myself a very adaptable person. I've done a lot of things that others probably wouldn't have allowed themselves to; I've bent in a lot of uncomfortable positions in order to get by. Passing time in the nothingness of poverty, such as looking for that needed cigarette when you have no change to go downstairs and buy a single at the liquor store, can be an entire afternoon's activity. So, yeah, I take a little sexual harassment from Todd here and there to feed my nicotine addiction, my inability to say no to hits of inspiration from his pipe, my allusions of friendship. Maybe I've learned to get by a little too well.

Not only must Todd die and slither away into the obscurity of my mind, but it must be me who kills him. Can't have anyone doing my dirty work for me. If I can't kill Todd, how will I be able to kill the other toxicities in my life? Larger, more toxic, front-and-center toxicities? I've realized I don't have a cold shoulder—that is, a limit to my compassion—as some of my friends like Sasha or Brahim might, which is why I am not yet extricated from this vulgar relationship. But is that a bad thing, limiting one's compassion?

Sometimes when I have spare time, I call Felicity to see if I can talk some of this stuff out with her. She doesn't answer my calls.

It's past nine o'clock at night and both my hands are full of bags. New underwear from Macy's. Prescriptions from CVS. Household items from the adjacent Target. It's drizzling but I can still see the moon. A night more wet than cold. Street and sidewalk traffic is light as I intently stride the final blocks home. Since no visible cars are coming, many pedestrians around me defy the red hand at the stoplight on Cyril Magnin and cross, while I wait for nothing.

On the last leg of Market before hitting Turk, I can already see him smoking a cigarette and dangling Zippy's leash from his limp fingers outside our building, bent over and broken-looking. *Fuck*, I think. I'll have to pass him to get in. As I gather my emotional strength and approach the entrance, Zippy senses me and bursts to life, stretching his leash to sniff and lick my hand as if I were holding food in my palm. "Hey Zippy," I say as a reflex while reaching for my keys, ready to jump for my life at even the mildest indication of confrontation. Todd has cut his hair short in just the same manner as I recently have. Even though he's averting his face, I can see he's been crying. "Hi Todd." Before I get to the door, he says something through tears that I can't gather. My brain does a double take: door, Todd, door, Todd crying and looking at me.

"I don't understand," he says. "Why-why won't you talk to me?" Droplets are running down his pale face.

I'm blinded by an explosion of rage. I'm mentally breaking glass, punching walls, and tearing whatever my nails will dig into. This is exactly the type of situation I was trying to avoid. I want to escape. I need to disappear, to run, but my legs won't jumpstart.

"Listen, Todd, life isn't fucking fair. We can't all get what we want," I shout in a hot-faced fury. "You think I started stalking my best friend Megan when I realized she had given me the slip? No." I lean in to hiss, "Things *suck*." Zippy huddles behind his owner, shielding himself from me. "I can't help you. Get it?" And then I leave him outside.

As I take the stairs up to my apartment, I can't shake the image of Todd standing in the rain—his sunken eyes; the lost, pouty look; his disheveled hair and wind-whipped, smudgy face—which engraves itself into my memory instantly and forever. As the "nice" guy, I'm not used to snapping like that. I'm not used to causing such reactions in people, either. I walk exhausted through my front door as a piercing flash of shame zaps me from underneath my toes to the back of my neck. *Have I made a mistake?* I wonder. *Am I some sort of criminal?*

I set down my bags and go to the bathroom, Todd's rain and tear-splattered face still plaguing me. After flushing the toilet, I catch sight of myself in the mirror over the sink. Something is hatched in my guts, the punch of love I imagine parents must feel for their newborns. It inflates until it fills all of me, suffocating me with its alien beauty.

I find my last, half-smoked cigarette in the ashtray and light it before digging around for the nicotine replacement therapy box and applying a patch: Step One.

poem

Painful Jewelry
caitlin mitchel-markley

And then there were those new bruises
the really deep and tender ones,
that were just high enough on my arm
so my short-sleeves covered them –
as long as I didn't raise my hand
otherwise, out would peek
that circle of indigo smudges
what a strange tattoo it would be
like five blurry blackberries
a shackle of fingerprints
wrapped around my bicep
always in the same spot
the spot where you would grab me
when I didn't move fast enough
when you were adding other bruises
when you would shake me,
as if to knock those berries off
but they never fall to the floor
they just sit there on my body
aching and fading
losing their purple depth
shifting to blue, then green, then yellow
such a beautiful blend of colors
it would be lovely bracelet
if it wasn't such painful jewelry

A Friend of the Family

heather whited

Great Aunt Mel had forgotten who she was again.

When I came into her room at the old folks' home with my weekly bunch of daisies and loaf of zucchini bread, she was sitting on her bed staring at herself in the mirror across the room, looking very pleased.

"I think Bobby is going to propose tonight," she said.

At first, this was no tipoff that she was so far gone. She and Grandma had both loved Bobby, my Granddad, after all. I went on putting the flowers in a vase for her while Great Aunt Mel cocked her head this way and that, admiring herself. About half of her lunch was cold, going to waste on a beige plastic tray sitting nearby. I reminded myself to check in and see if she was eating okay. She looked well enough, at the moment, was giving her reflection a coy pout.

"Melody is sure going to get her knickers in a twist!" my great aunt exclaimed with glee, tossing her silver hair, still thick and lustrous, over her shoulder.

This I could not take. I knew they had their differences, and Lord knows she wasn't perfect, but I loved my Grandma and not even her twin sister was going to say a word against her, or do some unflattering impression of her as a vixen.

I went to the bed and gently took her hands in mine. They were as frail and weightless as a pair of butterfly wings.

"You're not Trixie, Auntie Mel. Take a look."

Her watery eyes got large and scared as she took me in, and she scrunched up her face in the pained expression that told me she was trying her hardest to remember who I was. She walked with me to the mirror, and I turned on the lamp there.

There was a girl, Flora, who helped Auntie Mel in the mornings with dressing and fixing her hair and things. She was also a wiz at makeup and each day, she covered the long scar down Auntie's face and neck. The lamp's light wasn't enough though, so I took a bit of tissue and wiped off a portion of Flora's art, exposing the scar.

Auntie Mel saw then that she wasn't her twin sister after all. She raised her hands to her face and screamed, remembering everything.

Back home, I had things to do.

Our Friend was moping with the cat in the living room because I had been gone too long. Both followed me to the kitchen.

"What? Can't a lady get her nails done?" I said, putting down the groceries in a huff. Shelby cat rubbed against my legs. Our Friend hung back, chastised.

"I was seeing Auntie too, if you must know," I snapped at Our Friend. "Admiring your handiwork."

Our Friend understood sarcasm all too well. It bristled, but I gave it no sympathy and kept on taking vegetables from the paper bag.

"Let me be. Ben is coming for dinner. I want to get ready."

This got Our Friend's attention. It didn't like Ben at all, but watch it stop me from having him over. If Our Friend wanted another girl child to take care of it when I'm gone, it would have to let me. Since Momma did her duty, I was all there was. End of the line, as it were.

I started to feel bad as I cooked, a bit guilty about how I had spoken. There was a huge storm last week and Our Friend was a gem making sure we were the only house on the street with power. It found my rain boots that same morning and left them for me by the door. Our Friend did try.

I was introduced to Our Friend when I was five.

Momma chose my first day of kindergarten, which was also a week after Grandma did her duty and gave herself to it. She waited until Daddy had left for work. I was coloring in the living room and Momma was in the kitchen, taking a moment to herself. She made herself a black coffee and sat at the table, watching the rain hit the kitchen window. The house was so peaceful and still that I heard it clearly, each ping against the window and each little contented sigh Momma made and she sipped from her favorite mug, the one Daddy had bought her on their honeymoon trip to Dollywood.

"Jojo," said Momma. She put down her coffee. "Can you come here with me?"

I was happy to do whatever Momma asked, so I followed her to what we called Granddad's room, where he had lived with Grandma long before I was born. I was shocked when she got out the key that opened that room. We never went in there. The door opened easily though, not a creak or a groan.

Our Friend was waiting.

I was only five, so all the old blood stains on the walls and wood floor made me a bit squeamish, and Our Friend truly is a sight to behold, but it just bounded right up to me like a puppy, making me giggle and I never had a chance to get scared. I looked up at Momma and she smiled down at me. Momma was a collection of nice features, but her smile really took the cake, and this smile lit up her face, making her look even prettier than usual. She told me everything then.

"Daddy doesn't even know this room exists," Momma said when she'd gone over the basics. She had let Our Friend out to roam the house and it followed behind us, eager to get to know me. I helped Momma make my sandwich for lunch while Our Friend nuzzled at my hand, wanting me to pay it attention. "Our Friend just sort of keeps him from seeing, so you can't ever say anything. It would confuse Daddy and upset him and make a lot of work for Our Friend."

I agreed, delighted to have such an important secret to keep. Momma bagged up my lunch and helped me put on my raincoat and we walked together, hand in hand, down to the school. It was early September and the cold had come in early that year. Momma's round cheeks were red from the walk in the brisk air. With her sweet face and big eyes, people always thought her younger than she was. She talked to me in a low voice, smiling and waving at neighbors as we walked.

"And Daddy is going to go on thinking we had a funeral for Grandma too, so don't say anything now that you know she gave herself to Our Friend to make it nice and strong. You're my big girl, Jojo. You're one of us now."

Momma kissed me at the doorway to my classroom. Friendly Mr. Green with his soft sweater gave me a sticker with my name on it and showed me to my little desk. I was agog at all the day had brought. I was so glad I was five.

My first day at school, I drew a picture of Our Friend and there was a conference. Momma came without Daddy and smoothed things over with a story about a babysitter and an ill-advised scary movie. She brought zucchini bread and daisies with her. When I asked about the story she'd told my teacher, Momma said that she didn't like to lie at all, but sometimes a lie about Our Friend kept everybody safe, and that was more important.

"But the truth about everything else, all the time, Jojo," she said.

I learned to keep quiet. Our Friend was a great secret.

I never said anything and never had people over. Momma said it was easier than picking up the pieces should something go wrong. I was okay. I had Momma and Daddy and Daddy's dumb little dog, and I had Our Friend.

I got the stew going and ran myself a bath so I could freshen up before Ben got there. Our Friend was skulking around. Shelby lay in front of Our Friend, swatting and flicking her tail and trying to get it to play with her. Those two were thick as thieves.

"You hid from Ben last time he was over," I called out. "That can't go on forever. I won't let him wind up like Granddad, thank you very much. I don't want him like Daddy, either, gone without a dang trace. Can you please come out tonight? Can you help me?"

Our Friend made no promises. I knew it would prefer that there were no men around at all, but it understood it had to have them to get us, the women who took care of it and gave themselves to it to keep it strong.

While I was in the bath, the phone rang. I ran from the tub in my towel, dripping water all over the floor as I answered with a breathless hello.

"Hello. It's Flora. From the old folks' home."

"Oh, hello Flora."

I couldn't keep the excitement out of my voice and my heart sped up. She must have thought it was weird that I sounded so happy to hear from her because she only ever called when there was a problem with Auntie Mel.

"Hi Josephine."

"Jojo, please."

"Right. Jojo. Do you think you could visit twice this week? Miss Melody isn't doing too well. I just came back to help her with supper and she's really in a state."

"Well, sure, I'll come back over," I said. Luckily, or maybe unluckily, my brain was fast. "Why don't you stick around? I'll bring you some of my zucchini bread and maybe we can talk?"

I didn't know what I was doing at all, but it was terrible waiting for her answer. I drew the towel further up my chest, suddenly embarrassed to be talking on the phone while naked.

"Sounds good," she said. Her voice was warm. "Great."

I mumbled something about coming over Thursday and she said she'd see me then. I hung up the phone and realized I was blushing something fierce. Our Friend was staring at me.

"What? Can't a lady have a friend? Not everything is about you."

Daddy was, as I remembered him, a great man. Worked hard during the day, loved to take a walk with his dog in the evenings. Read to me every night. He was a good gardener, his and Momma's passion, with a pudgy stomach and all of three hairs on his head. People sometimes joked about how such a homely man with the physique of a lump of unrisen bread dough had gotten a pretty woman like Momma. To me, it was obvious, and I think it was to them too. It was the gentle way he did everything, the goodness that everyone noticed straight away.

I was ten when Momma sent him away.

Momma and I were as sad as we'd ever been to see him go and we both loved him, but it was time. He was making Our Friend sick and because he was, he was putting himself in danger.

She told me about the plan a week before, so I could be ready for it. Momma took over tucking me in that night and I looked up at her sitting on the edge of my bed, her hands folded in her lap after she made her announcement. I remember her that night in a soft flannel work shirt and worn corduroy pants rolled up at the ends. Her only jewelry was a thin gold chain and her wedding band. Instead of perfume, she smelled of baking and dish soap and the garden. Her nails still carried a bit of dirt underneath.

"What do you mean Daddy's going away?" I asked as I sat up in bed. In my room the wooden bed frame was an antique, something made by a family member years ago. Momma had sewn the quilt, yellow with a flower pattern, herself when she was a young woman, before she had even met Daddy. She had always known she would have a daughter. "Doesn't he love us anymore?"

"It's not that, Jojo," Momma said. She smoothed my hair and put a strand behind my ears. When we met eyes, she looked away. "It's not a matter of anyone not loving anyone. It's to keep Daddy safe."

It was something that had to be done so that Daddy didn't end up like poor Granddad all torn to bits when he stuck around too long. Momma told me she'd do it as kindly as possible. I knew why she had to do it, had to make him go away, but I still wasn't prepared for the day it happened.

Breakfast was normal but my stomach was in knots knowing what was about to happen. Daddy folded up his newspaper and said, "Gosh, it was getting late." Momma made sure to get my attention with a well-placed look. I knew it was time.

I gave Daddy a big hug and told him I loved him. Momma did the same, clutching at him, and we followed him to the door.

"What's all this?" he said. "I'm just going to work, not to Mars. Ha ha ha!"

He was the only one to laugh. I wrapped my arms around his legs and squeezed. At a look from Momma, I let go.

As he stepped outside, Our Friend came around the corner, staying unseen to Daddy. Momma took Daddy's face in her hands and kissed him on the cheek. There were tears in her eyes.

"Forget," she whispered into his ear.

It was a big favor to ask Our Friend, whose magic usually only reached as far as the door, but it worked. Daddy stood on the steps, staring at us.

"Excuse me, ma'am," he stammered, finding himself being held by a beautiful woman he didn't know. His face got red.

"No, excuse me," said Momma. She let him go. Behind me, Our Friend slinked away. I started to cry even though I had said I was going to be tough for Momma. I took off one of my shoes and threw it at Our Friend, who was just disappearing around the corner, looking exhausted and droopy.

Daddy backed away quickly, nearly tripping down the steps. The rosebush snagged his trouser legs and he reached down to pull the thorns away, still staring at Momma.

"So, so sorry. I don't know…I don't know whatever came over me."

He ran down the street. And that was the last I saw him.

Momma let me finish crying and never said a thing about me not being tough. To make up for what had happened, she took me to the animal shelter to get the cat I had always wanted but Daddy was allergic. I named her Shelby.

It took me until the day Momma did her duty, when I was ready to say goodbye to her, that I realized a few things about that day. The tears Momma held back for me that did not just last a moment, but that never left her eyes, the way her hands shook with the force of her grief as she went about making sure I was okay.

After she did her duty, I kept Momma and Daddy's empty room the same. There's a picture of the two of them on their wedding day by her side of the bed. The glass still carried a few fingerprints from where I guess she held it sometimes. She was beautiful with her hair long and a veil to her elbows. Daddy, his face red from nerves and the heat of a midsummer day, looked stunned at his good luck and about to burst from his suit. They both smiled like they'd never stop. And looking back on my childhood, they never did.

Momma never threw out a stitch of Daddy's clothes, or any of his books or even the oldest pair of ratty socks in the dresser drawer. I left Momma's things with his, and when I went in there to clean or visit, it was a sweet, warm feeling every time, like a lazy Saturday morning in fall with all of us together. It was one place I never let Our Friend go.

Before Ben arrived, I got out the box again.

It's where I kept all the family pictures and old jewelry and letters and other mementos. For months now, I'd been trying to tell Ben how things stood, but he just didn't see. I could only keep trying. If I was going to do this, I wanted him to know. I guessed we'd all done it a little different, all of us ladies in the family who took care of Our Friend, and this was going to be my way.

I set the table and then went outside to have a cigarette, which Ben didn't know about and I was happily going to keep that way. Shelby-cat followed me outside and stretched in the sun.

Our Friend ogled me out the window and I made a face.

"What? Can't a lady have a smoke? Jeez Louise!"

Maybe tonight I could get through to Ben. It had only been disasters so far, like the time I tried to show him Granddad's room. Before I'd even gotten to say a word about Our Friend and men being careful because it tore them to bits if it was around them too long, Ben had gone pale and shaky.

"Pardon my French, but what the hell is going on?" he said backing to the door. He stumbled and nearly fell to his rear.

I knew I'd made a mistake then. I had to call in a big-time favor and ask Our Friend to sort of take that memory away. Now, I knew to be careful. Start small. I guess the story of Granddad is a bad place to begin.

I finished my cigarette and went inside to check on the strew.

For the longest time, it was me and Momma. Daddy was gone and Grandma had done her duty when I was a little kid and it was just us two girls, as Momma said. And Daddy's dog, which we took care of and loved up to a ripe old age.

We were happy enough, and so was Our Friend. I could hardly believe this was the same Friend who mauled Auntie Mel's face sixty years ago when Grandma said she wanted her sister's boyfriend, the same Friend who tore Granddad apart right upstairs when it was given half a chance. It did so much for us, and we were always grateful.

Then, things started to change. It got sick from being without food for too long. It had been around fourteen years since Grandma, and Our Friend was suddenly starved. It made noises, kept us awake, left the water running, that sort of thing. A real nuisance. But it would get worse, we knew. Not just annoying things, but dangerous. So, Momma figured it was her time to do her duty. We were sitting outside having Cokes when she broke the news. I threw mine right against the wall and stomped inside.

Momma followed me to my room and wrapped her arms around me. She was so young still, only forty-two, and her beautiful hair only had the first strands of gray.

"It's going to be okay, Jojo. You'll see. This is so special and I'm very happy."

"It's too soon. It's not supposed to be time yet. It's been longer before."

"I know, sweetie. I know. I'm surprised too, but what can we do?"

I wiped my snotty nose on my shirt sleeve.

"It could be someone else…"

Momma pulled away from me. My face was already burning from embarrassment. I didn't mean it at all and knew it was a horrible thing to say.

"Never," said Momma. "We care for it, it cares for us, and when the time comes, we say thank you and do our duty."

"What would happen if you didn't? If you never did, or I never did?"

Momma got suddenly stern, sterner than she'd ever been before.

"That is not something you want to think about, Josephine. Now stop talking about Our Friend getting its food outside this house and us not doing our duty all that other nonsense."

Her expression softened again quickly, and she held me while I cried.

I wouldn't speak to Our Friend for days. It knew I was mad and tried to make up by bringing me little things and being helpful, but I was not buying it.

Momma said that after it had eaten, I could get whatever I wanted from Our Friend. It'd be in a good mood and strong and feeling bad for what had happened. I didn't want to think about that.

"It does love us, you know," Momma told me. "Our Friend loves us very much. Why, when Grandma did her duty, it was helping out in the days before, even weak as it was. Do you remember?"

I said that I didn't. Momma smoothed my hair and placed it behind my ear.

"I suppose not. Grandma was scared. No shame in that, Jojo. Remember. Well anyway, I asked her what would help and she said she remembered this record she used to dance to with Granddad and she'd love to hear it one last time. I had a talk with Our Friend and lo and behold if it hadn't found the record in a few hours. Grandma felt much better after."

I was unrepentantly petulant.

"What does that have to do with anything?"

Momma sighed and kissed me on the forehead.

"You'll see."

The day she chose came. Hot and sunny, her favorite weather.

Momma had a long bath and ate her favorite pizza, and we took a walk. She spent a little time alone in her room.

Our Friend hid in the basement all day.

At sunset, it was time. Momma hugged me tight and told me how proud she was of me. She reminded me how to wrap things up nice and official when she was gone. Then, she went downstairs and never came up. I lay on the couch and cried until I fell asleep. When I woke up, I called the police and told them my mother was missing. Then I went and made sure the basement wasn't a shambles.

It was a few days before I could look Our Friend in the face again. When I could, I told it what I wanted.

I wanted my dumb cat to live as long I did. No Momma, no Daddy, no friends to speak of, but I did have this cat, the only thing it seemed I'd get to keep besides a half-crazy great-aunt.

And Shelby-cat, already nearly ten years old at the time, hadn't been sick a day since. Fifteen years later and I was certainly no longer nineteen, but the cat was as youthful as could be. Credit where credit was due, I suppose.

I started taking care of Auntie Mel, which had always been Momma's job and before that, Grandma's. I learned the zucchini bread recipe and started to pick little bunches of daisies once a week.

One day last year, I went to visit and got the surprise of my life seeing Flora there making her presentable. She had long curly hair and a tiny diamond stud in her nose. She smiled when she introduced herself and my knees went weak. I started to wonder if maybe Momma wasn't right after all and things really would be okay.

Ben arrived with flowers and ice cream.

He was a good guy, Ben. I guess he reminded me a little of Daddy, all stomach and goofy smiles and kind eyes. If I had to have a girl baby with a man, I wanted it to be with a nice man, at least. Someone I could leave my little girl with good memories of, someone who'd take care of her when I'd done my duty. I was no spring chicken, as it were, and there was a good chance I'd have to do my duty when my little girl was small and she might need her daddy, whoever that ended up being.

Ben and I ate our dinner and then walked down to the little coffee shop on the corner and had ourselves some coffee before a stroll in the park.

Back home, I showed him the pictures in the box, hoping to ease into a conversation. All he had to say was what a shame it was about poor Auntie Mel's face and that she and Grandma really had been lookers.

Ben elbowed me playfully.

"Apple doesn't fall from the tree, heh, Jojo? Hey, how about that! Your family is a whole line of girls, isn't it? Just one or two every generation."

"There's a reason for that—"

"Of course," Ben beamed. He winked up at the ceiling, like God was in a joke he was making. "There's a reason for everything."

I tried something different.

"Haven't you ever wondered why I said I could only ever live here?"

Ben kissed my hand.

"You're a bit sentimental. I like that about you. Now, don't you want to play Monopoly?"

"Jeez Louise," I muttered under my breath. But I got out the game.

Ben fell asleep on the couch after ice cream and halfway through the first round.

I called softly for Our Friend.

"Please. Let me at least try? Let me try to see how this works. You know I'll never leave you."

I heard it creeping up the stairs.

"Please," I said again.

Ben began to stir. Our Friend hovered in the hallway, and I motioned it further into the room.

About the time it reached the end of the couch, Ben opened his eyes. His lips opened in a silent scream.

"There's someone I'd like you to meet," I said.

Night Patrol

deanna tibbs

My daughter's body is soft against me. She snuggles closer as we look down on the sidewalk and wait for something to happen, for anything to connect us to the rest of the world, if only in our minds. Our temperaments were already anxious, and the shelter-in-place order unlocked a dystopian readiness in us. It's been six days since we last went down the front steps. I imagine the air outside to be filled with a gaseous assailant, but the air inside to be safe. The backyard must be neutral because we spend time there without worry.

A silver sedan pulls up and parks in the middle of the street, hazards on. A man wearing a surgical mask gets out and takes a tightly packed plastic bag from the passenger seat and up to our neighbor's door. Dinner time. A few minutes later, a pack of kids kick their scooters by. They laugh with mouths—uncovered and wide open—an echo of a neighborhood turned ghost town.

"Why do they get to play together, mama?"

I tighten my arms. Inhale. I never get tired of the smell of her. I wonder how many more moments like this we will have, whether we will be able to maintain this closeness as she becomes a tween. "Different families have different rules."

"It's not fair."

"I know," I say unequivocally.

A Golden Retriever sniffs around the tree at our curb. The patch is full of weeds; foxtails will be a problem soon. A masked couple waits patiently for the dog to finish.

"They must have gotten those masks for the smoke last summer," I say. "They're sold out now. It's just a supply bottleneck, though. They'll be back." Years ago, I learned that the more utterances a baby heard from their primary caretaker, the higher their vocabulary would be as an adult, justifying my nature as an over-sharer. Shelter-in-place has brought a new quiet to our lives. Sentences and conversations are punctuated by prolonged and weary silences.

"I want a dog, mama. Ava, Sienna, and Max all got dogs. It's not fair."

I lightly rub her back. "I know," I say again, gently this time.

Seeing my daughter live through COVID-19 reminds me of the fears that I grew up with, though it was a very different predator who lurked outside of my window.

In the late 70's, before blue-collar workers fell from grace, my dad had a good job with Pacific Telephone and my mom stayed at home. California was experiencing unprecedented economic growth, which meant that Santa Cruz was becoming more expensive while a housing boom in the Central Valley drew families like mine inland. My parents bought a newly built cookie-cutter home and we relocated to the sprawl of suburban Sacramento.

In our first months in that house, my brother and I were tiny and unselfconscious explorers in the frontier of the partially developed housing tract. We'd put on our galoshes to stomp in the "lake," which was a very large puddle outside our front door, later to be leveled and paved into the road. Houses in the framing stage stood like dinosaur skeletons. When the crews were gone, we'd smell the fresh pine and collect sawdust curls in waning light. By the end of that year, construction was complete and new neighbors filled the homes.

We chose bedroom sets from the Sears catalogue. My selection was straight out of a fairy tale: a white four-poster canopy bed adorned in cotton candy pink gingham, a matching desk and bureau featuring gingerbread trim. Getting that musky cedar furniture is my first memory of owning something store-bought and new. My most cherished clothes back then were made by my mother. She would cut material from a pattern sprawled across our dining room table, then complete them on her Singer—a machine that she would fold in and out of a side table like a magic trick.

My room had a picture window overlooking several acres of pasture. (I would later credit the hours that I watched the cows graze for my early conversion to vegetarianism.) A few blocks away, there was a larger plot of open space being held vacant as a future park site. The setting was idyllic and by many measures our house and my life were pictures of the American Dream.

My mother made sure that my shade was closed at dusk. By night, my window was transformed into a portal for scary things. Our windows could not be thick enough, our doors could not be strong enough, and we could not check our locks too many times. Around the time that we moved in, the East Area Rapist committed eight attacks within three miles of our new residence. He was known for extensive planning of his crimes and eluding capture through creative escapes. The field behind our house and future park site were the types of open space property that he used to flee, making our new home an ideal target.

Every few months, I was woken by the sound of a police helicopter that would hover between those open spaces. My parents installed flood lights and my blinds would glow with cold light. Sometimes my mom would sit with me and encourage me to sleep, but I would lay alert, with my eyes wide and dry. Occasionally, she would peel back the edge of the shade, where she'd only find our empty yard, blanched and stark under artificial light.

Sketched faces of suspects became a presence in our living room almost as familiar as that of Beaver Cleaver or Gilligan. I learned untimely vocabulary and geography from the names that permeated the news: East Area Rapist, Original Nightstalker, Golden State Killer. Our television was on all day while we completed our homework, played with our pet rats, or ate dinner, offering background to all activities. I imagined that shaggy-haired, vacant-eyed man wandering my neighborhood while I slept.

Violence and fear were not unfamiliar to my household, but the domestic menace of my father was accepted. His low-level everyday danger paled in comparison to the man on the television—drawn in charcoal, forlorn and angry. There may have been comfort in accepting my father who was large and scary but knew how to use the shotgun hidden on the second shelf of the closet, when there was a more dangerous and less predictable man to fear.

I had a recurring nightmare that it was Halloween. While trick-or-treating with my brother, a fog and silence overtake the street. Other children vanish leaving my brother and I alone. When we turn, we see a green and stitched Frankenstein coming after us. We drop our pillowcases and run. My brother lags behind and after half a block, I can tell the monster is close behind me. I dive under a car and wait with panicked breath. When Frankenstein's square head peeks underneath the car and the monster's eyes meet mine, I wake with a start.

A few years passed and news of the serial killings waned. My father started taking Prozac and got into New Age ideas, which helped his anger subside.

We would occasionally receive hang-up phone calls. One time, the caller stayed on the line while I said, "Hello? ... Hello?"

My mom was stirring her signature marinara on the stove. She dropped the wooden spoon and came to the counter near where I held the phone. She leaned in close, tense and serious. "Was there breathing? Did you hear anyone breathe?" she asked urgently.

"No, there was nothing but silence."

"That's what he does to people," she said, and I knew who she meant.

My brother and I planned an April Fool's Day prank on her. April first fell on a Sunday, the day that she always slept in. We got up at first light and taped black garbage bags to the sliding glass door of her room in an attempt to keep the light from coming in, hoping she would continue to think it was nighttime. We had my father change the time on the clock in their bedroom. The trick backfired when she panicked that someone was tampering with the door. She was dialing 911 when my dad called us inside to put an end to it.

My brother and I spent another long summer with little structure, most of it indoors, as playing out on the street was unbearable in the valley heat, regularly topping 100. I studied and tracked TV commercials as a hobby. I could beat any winner of The Price is Right given the chance. We biked to the Circle K for candy or got a popsicle from the ice cream truck wailing its warbly "Turkey in the Straw." We took our ten speeds to the park site for off-road riding. Oak trees provided shade making the temperature bearable.

My brother asked me if I wanted to come along on Night Patrol, a game that he'd been playing with neighborhood friends. We wore black clothes under our pajamas, and he set the alarm on his digital watch. He woke me when it was time and handed me a flashlight. I followed him through his room, up and over his desk and out the window, onto the crate placed inconspicuously along the side of the house.

He had a backpack with snacks on his shoulders and a baseball bat in his hands. We went through our side gate to the sidewalk to meet neighborhood friends. I felt the thrill high in my stomach, my cheeks burning red, sweating and shivering at the same time. As we neared the top of our block, my brother hit the metal light pole with the bat for fun. It resonated like a gong. Adrenaline shot through me, and we all bolted around the corner until our hearts returned to normal. We walked ten minutes to the future park site to tell ghost stories, holding our flashlights so they shined up from the bottom of our chin like we'd done at camp, or maybe seen in a movie.

After a few of these outings, summer was coming to a close. We went out one more time on a Friday night after school had resumed, but it was harder with a schedule to keep. Then, our mom told us that we could no longer visit the park site for bike rides. Homeless folks had moved in. It went unspoken, but the Night Patrol had run its course.

Long after we had grown, we told our mother about our night outings. My brother laughed at how warped the screen on his bedroom window had become due to the wear of taking it out and putting it back in.

"I remember that screen," my mother said. "I thought it might be a sign that the Nightstalker had tried to get into our house."

When she said it, I realized that I had never considered what she had endured as a woman or as a parent while navigating the reality of a serial rapist preying on our region. For us kids, it was a fact of life that we adapted to. We were scared when there were helicopters, but we were regular kids the rest of the time. The events had become a part of history, long ago tucked into our subconscious. For my mother, the fear permeated her daily life and shaped her adulthood.

"I never felt safe in that house," she said.

In 2015, I listened to an eleven-part podcast that described the Golden State Killer's attacks in detail. I'd never heard the incidents laid out in methodical macabre detail, but it was familiar, stored in a nimble place of my brain where packages of memory could unfold neatly once untied. My husband and daughter were out of town, and I felt the solitude in my bones while I listened. Every night, I walked around my house checking and rechecking window and door locks. The fear was visceral, like he had been a part of my life all along.

I got online and did some googling. It wasn't until then that I realized how close many of his crimes were to my childhood home. The Nightstalker had personified the fear that I lived with during that time, but he was not the only serial killer that had been nearby in my youth. Historians mark the late 60s to the early 90s as the heyday for serial killers, which precisely spans my entire childhood. Sacramento and the Bay Area were a home to many of them.

In 2018, Joseph James DeAngelo, aka The Original Nightstalker, aka the East Area Rapist, was arrested. He had been living within miles of the majority of his crimes, and just a few miles from my childhood home. Investigators used DNA evidence to do genetic tracing via a popular website and found close genetic relatives to pinpoint their suspect. Since his arrest, articles covering the case and his court proceedings always catch my attention and often provoke a text with my mother. Now we track him again, but for the first time can put that fear to rest.

Ten days ago, George Floyd was suffocated while being arrested and racial justice protests have erupted worldwide. The last two days have been hot, signaling the beginning of fire season. Every day I go around opening and closing windows based on incremental changes in the sun and wind. Living in the heat and dark feels oppressive.

At night, I lay in bed under a thin sheet with my daughter to chat before she falls asleep. She started sharing my bed when school closed. I don't mind. She spends so much of her time alone now, she doesn't have to sleep alone, too. I hear helicopters circling over Downtown Oakland. There are riots, but we do not feel unsafe. We have the windows open now to let in the cooling bay breeze.

"When will things go back to normal?" she asks.

I swallow and am bombarded by thoughts. I know she is talking about coronavirus, but I can't help but think about white supremacy, the environmental crisis, all of the bleak unknowns facing her generation. Pandemic homeschooling has stretched relationships in my family. I'm ashamed at how reactive I have become, bypassing compassion for anger—an ugly shadow of my father that lives with me. Loving her is not enough to keep my daughter safe from my history, from this world.

I am finally able to speak, but my voice breaks. "Some people think this is a good time to change normal, to build a world that is better than normal."

She puts one arm around my neck and cups my chin with the other. "It will be okay, Mommy. It will."

We become quiet, my arm draped over her side and feel her breath become more slow and steady until I feel the twitch that signals her entry into sleep. I get up and close windows throughout the house. When I get to her bedroom, I see a possum frozen at the sight of me. Then I look further down and see a crate, sitting next to the house. I think to myself that I'll have to remember to move that.

The Peril at the Center of What Feeds You

allisa cherry

All over the tree, perfect figs
absorb wasp corpses
and get ready. Their flesh
dimples at the sight of your fingers.
A throaty scent rises
all around you, its density
convinces you that
you are still a beauty,
transformed by dusk
and the polleny dust that lies
over the orchard's stillness.
But listen,
deep in this sweetness
the ghost of a wasp buzzes.
It has left this barb
for your throat:
a memory
of the first time your body
spanned the bench
of a young man's pickup
and you met him, mouth to mouth.
You were parked
beneath an old mulberry.
The town was parched in drought
but you poured
toward a certain way of knowing
while discs of light,
tossed through the moving boughs,
illuminated sun drunk bees
making lazy infinity signs
in the dapple. You were hunting
for a fullness that wouldn't come
when a strong wind rose
and the tree gave up its ripest berries.
They fell as red and heavy
as blood clots across the bed
and the roof and the windshield.

fiction

The One Who Got To Stay
nancy hill

Five hours
Didn't think I'd ever come back here, but it's the right place to be. Took nearly a half-an-hour driving up and down the dozen or so streeets that make up this town to find a place I would't be noticed. I credit being good at what I do to that very lesson: invisibility equals freedom. Your exact words.

Funny how many of your words I remember even though we haven't spoken for years. Or written. Or shared any words in any way other than in my head, me doing the talking for both of us. Closer to fifty years than forty.

Sometimes the conversations are hostile. Angry. Me demanding over and over, "How could you? How could you? How could you?" You believed in mercy killing. War taught you that. I understood. But mercy killing for a person young and healthy? What sense in that?

Usually our exchanges in my head are full of long silences. Understanding passing between us with no need for words. Nice and easy. Safe.

The houses are no better off than when we called this town home. Here and there you can see evidence that somebody tried improvements—or at least did what needed to be done to keep a house from sinking into the ground. A patched roof. Paint slapped over peeling paint. Windows boarded over so rain can't get in.

Ratty blankets or stained bedsheets half cover windows. Yards mutilated with broken toys. A pair of houses have old washing machines turned on their sides near a towering hedge they share. Three have toilets converted into planters full of dead flowers that might have lived a rainy season at the most. A few have old bedsprings serving as fences. Almost every place has a car on cinderblocks that might be worked on some day. One has a bus all shiny in the sun with both sides and the backend painted with messages promising salvation.

I pause in front of a giant oak in one of the yards–do you remember it? It would be worth photographing again (remember when you did that?) if it wasn't surrounded by broken bikes on three sides and an old couch half-covered with weeds on the other. Some photographers make a name for themselves taking pictures of such things, which I find pretty worthless. Not that I look for beautiful sunsets over mountain ranges or close-ups of pretty flowers full of pollen, but I know the photographers taking pictures of these sorry yards think they're capturing some slice of America. But that can't be done without people in them. We're more than our possessions. Some people can't be bothered with how things look because there are too many bigger things going on in their lives to occupy their time.

I come to an empty lot full of old cans and bottles, a few mismatched shoes, black plastic bags full of trash. Rain barrels with more holes than metal take up the space where we used to live. It probably didn't take much to knock down that sweet little cabin we called home. Whether it fell by nature or human hands is hard to say. Although if I was the betting kind, I'd say it was human hands. Souvenir hunters most likely.

Maybe our house was on the small size, but it fitted us just fine. We didn't have much to begin with and we were happy to sit close to each other. We liked the way each other smelled. We said as much several times a day.

I close my eyes and inhale, as if the scent of you when you pulled up beside me all those summers ago still hangs in the air. Both of us on that lonely road. You in your gray, rusted-at-the-edges Karman Ghia. A classic, you liked to say. Never once did either of us see it as the beater it really was.

"Where you headed?" were the first words out of your mouth. You'd pushed the tan toothpick you were chewing aside to ask me. It dangled from the corner of your mouth like the world's skinniest cigarette.

"Got me," I said. The road I was walking on could be leading nowhere for all I cared. I hadn't expected to meet anybody on it, to tell you the truth.

"Well, isn't that a coincidence? I'm going to Got Me myself. Climb on in."

You pushed the passenger seat up and I thought you wanted me to crunch myself into that empty space where a seat might be in the back, but no, you wanted me to stash my old army backpack I'd taken from my uncle's attic back there. I wondered if my uncle noticed it was missing yet. He'd miss that long before he missed me.

I climbed in beside you. You pointed to a bag of peaches on the floor. "Help yourself," you said. So I opened the bag and out jumped that wonderful smell I keep tucked in my memory for times I forget there's good in this world. I almost didn't have to eat the peach to taste it, the smell shouting everything those sweet peaches were about. Your scent—wild and bold, sweet and tangy—likewise told me everything I needed to know about you.

Thinking of that day makes me crave a peach. But it's too early in the season for them. Still I can almost taste them just remembering that bag of them at my feet in your gray, rusted-around-the-edges Karman Ghia.

Maybe I should have been scared of you—a good-looking stranger wearing faded jeans with a paisley patch on the thigh closest to where I was sitting in the passenger seat, your long hair blowing in the breeze coming through the car window, but not for one minute was I ever fearful of you. Were the other girls, I wonder. I doubt it. You aren't the kind to be scared of.

For three days we let miles pass us by, more open road waiting just up ahead, stopping only to sleep at night. We shared your sleeping bag since I hadn't one of my own. It was mighty cozy. I knew you might want to do more than sleep since we were pressed close together and I could feel your excitement, but you didn't make any moves. Anyway, it was me who started things. I wanted to know what it felt like to have somebody I liked inside of me instead of those other men my daddy sent to my room, relatives among them, who I couldn't stand. I was a moneymaker for my family. Not that I'm proud of how I did it, but at least I more than paid my way and put plenty of food on the table, which is more than some could say. The worst of those men smelled like they used grease rags instead of toilet paper to clean themselves after they did their business.

Four hours

I'm at the inner blocks of town now, having started at the outside and worked my way through. The last house I pass before turning the corner has a big yard and off to one side is the littlest motorcycle I've ever seen. Toddler size. I'll bet he'll be a motorcycle riding rodeo star when he grows up. Or she. If they do. Grow up that is. That doesn't always happen in tiny towns like this as I've learned from experience.

When I round the lopsided corner, the houses get closer together. They're smaller than the ones on the outer streets, but the yards are bigger. Still, bigger yards or not, there's no privacy in these houses on account of windows and doors being left wide open to let fresh air in. You wouldn't like that. Privacy was important to you. We don't want people paying too much attention to us, you told me from the get-go.

"Why's that?" I asked. One of the many good things about you was that you didn't much mind me asking questions, something few people in my life had tolerated up to then.

"'Cause what if they take you away from me?"

"That won't happen. I walked out of the house I grew up in and down the road the day I turned eighteen. There's nothing anybody can do about it. My life's all one hundred percent my own now."

Neither of us had much to say about what went on in our lives before your Karman Ghia stopped for me. Looking back wasn't a good idea for either of us. Both of us had sons of bitches for fathers, mothers long since gone, and between us, the only relative either of us had worth a damn had been your twin sister who hung herself when she was fourteen, long before I came into your life.

"Best thing that ever happened to her," you said. And I knew what you meant without asking for details. Which I wouldn't have done since I could tell the loss of her pained you, even if it had been for the best. I suspect her life might have been a lot like mine when it came to earning money to help the family out.

This town sure is full of American flags. Some hang from trees and some poke out of the ground on sticks and poles of all kinds of what-have-yous. There are probably hundreds of flag decals on car and truck fenders and hanging them from porches seems a popular way to show your love for America.

Remember when I stole a flag off a mailbox and sewed it onto your favorite pair of jeans? It was the one and only time I saw your eyes turn cold.

"You can't go stealing things." Your voice came out so low and fierce I could barely make out the words. "It'll draw attention to us and that's just nothing we can tolerate."

At the time I thought this was some more behavior you had learned in Vietnam where you had come back from a few years before you picked me up in your gray Karman Ghia. In Vietnam, you told me, you were as good as dead if you were seen. "Everybody was. On both sides. Or worse, you'd be left alive wishing you were dead. There were ways to take care of such things." I could tell that troubled you. I wanted to reassure you that you weren't in a jungle anymore, but I held that thought for another time. You could roll into yourself so deep I couldn't find you if you thought about the past too long.

Later that day we drove around until we found a swimming hole just outside of town. Hardly anybody risked swimming there because it was death itself begging you to jump in. The water ran wild no matter what time of year and the rocks surrounding it were high and jagged. Irregular. Being reckless demands a price. I'm heading there now.

Three hours and counting

When I'm nearly to the dirt road that leads to the waterfall, I see a goat woman. These little towns almost always have an old woman who lives with goats. I never have figured out why that is, but I hope it never changes. The goats are sitting atop an old chicken coop with the old woman. Her white hair is the exact shade of the goats' beards. I slip back behind a thick tree to listen to her play her flute for them. The silver of her long instrument shoots off sparks of light perfectly timed to the notes she plays. I can't help but think what a beautiful picture it would make, the sun shining just at the right angle to light up the edges of the woman's hair and the profile of the goats, their beards light as clouds, but the moment is so sacred that this will be one of my favorite pictures—the kind that just live forever in my head for me alone to look at when the darkness sets in.

You taught me about those kinds of pictures. "Some things are meant only to live inside of us," you'd explained once when we came across a field of wild irises at sunset, the purples and blues of the irises against the red and orange of the sunset proving differences show beauty in a way sameness never can. "Leave some things for other people to discover," was another way you looked at not taking every picture you came upon.

Later when your pictures and all those negatives became part of evidence, I knew there were other reasons not to record things. Although the newspapers never published those pictures out of respect for those whose lives you took, they never hesitated to mention that the pictures of those dead girls were remarkable tender.

Two hours and counting

The waterfalls we found down the dirt road close to town are still something to behold. Drought hasn't made the narrow gush of water any slower and the rocks jutting out every which way above and below the falls would still take a life in a heartbeat if someone were to slip and fall or maybe just throw themselves over for reasons only they would understand. Crows still call out overhead as they shout out nonsense to each other.

On our first day here we stumbled upon this place, tucked back off the road behind trees hundreds of feet high and growing so close together you'd think they couldn't get enough of each other.

You had your camera with you like always. We were at the bottom of the falls. It took a while to get down there, but neither of us shied away from danger. We got to the base to take a dip in the water that bubbled beneath it. The sun came through the trees, casting shadows that moved with the water, and we stripped down to bare skin knowing nobody would likely to see us. We'd have heard them coming, anyway. Just as I ventured in, all the sudden you tossed your shirt to me and told me to put it on.

"Leave it unbuttoned and tie the tails right at the top of your thighs."

I got your shirt wet which I hadn't meant to do. You didn't get mad but instead said that was perfect.

"Wander into the water some," you said. This was tricky since there was no way of knowing when the rock I'd been standing on might drop off and I'd be over my head in a flash, but I did what you asked. I could swim, so nothing to worry about.

You started taking pictures one after another and when you got them developed, for the first time in my life, I saw myself as beautiful.

You were good at that. Making me look beautiful. When I asked how you managed to turn a plain Jane like me into a beauty, you explained there's beauty in most everyone if somebody doesn't go and spoil it first. And it helps if you learn how to spot it. Beauty, that is.

You turned to me, frowning, and said, "You're the very first one I met that managed to hold on to it. Beauty, I mean." You pulled me close for one of your tender kisses, the kind that made my heart glow with an unearthly light.

One late night when it was too hot to breathe you brought up your notion of beauty again. "Until I spotted you walking down that lonesome road away from troubles, I believed that once beauty was stolen, all that was left was misery. I saw plenty to prove I was right about that, and I set about sparing others that misery. But then there you were, proving me wrong without saying more than 'Got me.'"

You turned so serious then I barely breathed. The moonlight came through the window, shining in the whites of your eyes. You said the strangest thing then that took me years of conversations with you in my head to understand and I never did get a chance to tell you that I knew why you did what you did. "You turned me into a selfish son of a bitch. I hope you'll forgive me when the time comes."

The way you looked then is one of those pictures that is purer in my heart than on a roll of film. It never needs to become something any other living person needs to see.

I have my own camera now. It's around my neck, like always. But there isn't anybody or anything that needs photographing right now. I've been taking pictures myself since you gave me your camera at the last minute.

Now the whole reason I'm considered good and some people even collect my pictures is because I remembered what you said that day about finding the beauty if you know how to spot it. I'm here to tell you that I've learned to find beauty with very little trouble at all. And one thing I wonder is if things would have been different for you if you weren't so good at spotting it yourself.

Earlier on, while I listened to the goat woman play her flute, I said something about darkness. This was something you knew all about. We'd talk about it, you and me, and you warned me you'd done some very bad things and you didn't know if it was the darkness that made you do bad things or if the bad things had created the darkness. I asked what sort of bad things and you said things bad enough to get you locked behind bars for a long time.

"Things you did in the war?" I asked. I wanted you to stop worrying about prison if that was the case because people didn't get put in prison for what happened in wars.

"Some in the war. Some afterwards. Some before, but not too many things before. But don't worry. I don't expect to do bad things anymore now that there's a you in the world and somebody, namely me, to protect you. It's just taken me a while to get things figured out."

"What sort of things?"

You thought this over and shook your head. "Hard to explain. Even to myself. Something about there being bad and good for everybody. Nobody gets spared and only a fool tries to go against the laws of that. Guess you could say it took me a while to get my head straight on that."

That was more than you usually said at any one time. You seemed embarrassed by it, so I tried to lighten things up. I dropped my head from one shoulder to the next, holding both hands out so the thumbs and index fingers of each hand made right angles. "Your head looks pretty straight to me," I teased. You never minded being teased.

"Hold it just like you are," you said. So I did and you grabbed your camera off the floor, which you kept by the door, and took my picture. It was a fine camera, which you told me about one night when it was too hot to sleep and the perfect temperature for mosquitos to buzz symphonies in our ears. You got the camera from a friend in Vietnam. Seems he'd been shot in the middle of the street and couldn't make it until the medics came to rescue him, even though you tried to keep the blood from flowing from the hole in his stomach. You were there with him, the two of you at the end of the forty-eight hours you'd been free to go into town to find some refreshments as you called them, meaning drugs and maybe girls.

It never bothered me any to hear about the girls since they were hookers whose families were probably dead and they needed to earn a living the best way they could. You and your friend had met two girls the night before and went into a little cramped space separated by big pieces of cardboard taped together with special army tape they'd found somewhere. Business done and over with, you left the girls and went out in search of more fun.

The next morning the girls found you again, but you were out of money. Usually then you'd be left alone, but those girls didn't believe you. They kept after you and your friend until you stepped around them and told them to go away. Then just like that, the shorter one pulled out a gun invisible under her clothes and shot your friend.

Last thing he said was to take his camera and just like that, you learned how to take pictures. They were good. Real good. I should know since I've been a photographer ever since they took you away, nearly fifty years ago now. When I send my secret photographer agent pictures, she sells them for oodles of money. Even she doesn't know my real name or where to find me, but she knows my post office box and will not betray that information so anyone can track me down because she knows that part of what makes my pictures worth so much is that my identity is a mystery. I like it that way. I will keep it that way. Who wants to be the one who got away? I found that out faster than the shutter clicks on a bright sunny day.

One hour and counting

I perch at the top of the waterfall and think about that. Being the one that got away. That's what the detective and others kept saying after they arrested you in the small house we lived in not far from where I am now. You were right about going to prison for a long time. Forever, as it turns out. They gave you the death penalty since you killed all those girls. Took me the longest time to figure out why you would do something like that.

We'd been lying in bed, sheets and legs all tangled. There was no knock or even a warning shout that somebody was coming in. You and me all part of the same moment, side-by-side, my head on your chest. The same position we always got in before we fell asleep. Our serious sleeping position as you called it.

You shoved me to the floor and rolled on top of me. Grabbed the clock off the three-legged table we used for a nightstand, the fourth leg being a stack of used paperbacks from the general store in town.

You threw the clock and covered my ears to block who knows what, although I read in the newspapers that your very kind public defender who tried everything to get you a not guilty verdict—although there was no hope of that ever happening—said you thought the clock was a hand grenade and you were back in the war. The newspaper also reported that you laughed when he said that and the judge had to bang his gavel down and shout, "Order in the court."

I wasn't at the trial. I went to visit you as soon as they'd let me, which was almost a week after they stormed in on us, and you told me not to go to your trial or to visit you because reporters would give me no peace. I respected your wishes but I read every word ever written about you, which you had also advised me against. I saw you one more time—in court when I was subpoenaed and I told the truth and whole truth and nothing but the truth about your gentle nature. I kept saying they'd made a terrible mistake over and over until the judge said I'd made my point and move on.

That was the one and only time I saw you again after they locked you up. They found you guilty of killing eight girls. They only knew about six until they looked at all your pictures. Then they counted eight. They were all teenagers. All running away from something. Just like me. All happy to take the ride you offered.

You promised there were no more and that if there were, you would admit it since now that the truth was out, you wanted their families to know you'd done it to spare them anymore pain. "You know what I'm talking about, motherfuckers," the newspapers reported you'd shout-ed into the packed courtroom. They said you'd looked half-mad. They meant crazy. I knew you weren't that kind of mad.

That was when I understood what you meant by being selfish. You maybe had thought to end my pain, too, when you first picked me up, but then what we had was so beautiful that you didn't want to let me go, even if it meant I would know more of the pain of living.

You told me not to write to you and wouldn't put me on your ap-proved visitor list either. If it weren't for what was between us, that would have killed me. But I understood.

You got the death penalty, but what with one appeal and another, you lasted until the death penalty was declared unconstitutional in the state where you were serving your time and then your sentence was changed to life in prison without possibility of parole.

After that a big important writer got a huge award for a book about you. I read it. There were a lot of things in it about you that I knew noth-ing about. Being in a war was the least of the pain you knew.

There were also a lot of things that weren't in the book. I'd never thought they were secrets until that book came out. Big things. Important things, like how you were way more than the bad things you did. But nobody wanted to hear that, so what was the point of sharing it?

One part of the book stuck with me. Once when the writer visited you in prison, he asked you if you had killed those young girls all because of the woman killing your friend in Vietnam. You said not to your recollection. The reporter must have kept harping on that—probably because so many psychologists who had never met you offered that opinion in court—and finally you said, "Listen, it was messed up that some girl shot my friend, but I wasn't trying to get even or anything like that. It was war. War is just like that. War lets in the bad just like love lets the good in. I insist you quote me on that."

I knew this was your message to me. The only one you ever sent.

One minute and counting

I came here because it was as close as I can get to you, the person I loved, and who loved me back when they shovel your ashes into the ground. I know the exact time because the newspaper reported it. Your natural life ended the day before yesterday. You, an old man found dead of natural causes in your prison bed. Old or not, I'd have recognized you. And you would have known who I was even if you were blind.

They even had a service for you—for your ashes, I should say—although probably the only people who went were reporters and the strange kind of people who like to follow these things, the same people who tore our small house apart for souvenirs. You'll be buried in the prison cemetery, marked by your inmate number.

As I stand on the edge of the waterfalls, I think about the day we discovered this place that's full of both beauty and peril. I close my eyes and remember how you saw beauty in me and taught me to seek beauty, too. I imagine the pictures still waiting for me to find, and I hold the pictures of you that live only in my head. Clear, beautiful images of you driving the gray Karman Ghia and rescuing me from my past, of the look on your face as you entered me the first time, of us tangled in sheets, of the expression as you looked through the viewfinder of your camera every day when you took my picture, of you showing me love for the first time in my life, of the fleeting smile meant for me alone the last time I saw you, the smile that let me know the beauty in your heart.

Others saw a monster once they caught you. I never saw that, but I spent many sleepless nights trying to make sense of what you did. Maybe you thought you were saving those girls, but I hope you figured out the only thing you were saving was your confused idea that taking their lives was better than letting them do what they had a right to do with their own breathing, living selves. Like the goat woman playing her flute on top of the goat shed, everybody's life holds breathlessly still for moments of wonder.

I step away from the waterfall, ease back down on a wet jagged rock, and wait until night comes so I can gaze up at the starry sky and thank those stars that I wasn't the one who got away.

I was the one who got to stay.

After Contemplating a Photo of George Bernard Shaw's Revolving Writing Hut

linda malnack

I bring my heart. You bring a hammer.
We turn the house on its axis to face East.

I bring a cast iron pot. You bring hot coals to make a fire.
Together we turn the house South.

I bring a camera. You make a scene.
We make a child together. The house turns itself West
and sun spills over the threshold.

I fill a cup. You put a bag on the table.
A cold wind enters the house with blue eyes and a lifted skirt.
The fire blows out.

Lies are out of the bag, flying, dying on windowsills,
spinning with their legs in the air.

You raise your hammer. The baby wakes and screams.
You steal the camera. Leave.

The Winds come to console me, one by one.
West jiggles the baby on his knee.
South rekindles the fire.

East mends my heart with *Yes* glue, while North insists
repeatedly and annoyingly it was all his fault.

Cold Swim Home

cp bruno

The South End Rowing Club in San Francisco is so old that Ulysses S. Grant was in office when it opened. It is located at the North End of San Francisco, having circumnavigated the city by barge and is now the South End of nothing. Three types of open water swimmers belong there:

1. Those who kick my ass.
2. Those who cannot believe I beat them, and,
3. "Please, God, don't let them pass me."

John Flahavan was in the kick-ass category.

In fact, he kicked the asses of the swimmers who kicked my ass. Which was notable because he overcame immutable laws of fluid mechanics by propelling a body at speeds solely reserved for the lithe, the streamlined, and the elongated.

John was none of these things.

John was not built like the proverbial brick shithouse—no. John was built like the *bricklayer* of the proverbial brick shithouse. My opportunity to observe John swimming in quarters closer than any other South Ender allowed me to discern his hidden secret of speed: water feared him. At the molecular level individual hydrogen molecules, learning from their chlorinated or salinated brethren that John Flahavan was about to smash an atom with his stubby outstretched arm, dissipated quickly before him, projecting him forward to their equally frightened kin. Thus, John transported in pool and bay upon a bed of frightened sub-atomic ball bearings, sliding at high velocity toward shore or coping while the rest of us had to actually swim.

For South Enders who have had a hypothermic experience swimming in sub-fifty-degree water (necessitating the rapid appearance of emergency personnel), the decision to swim the New Year's Day Alcatraz with their Dolphin Club neighbors—MAGA to their BWM—is cause for concern. The two adjoining clubs—there is a secret passageway connecting them—can be differentiated in this way: The South End's unofficial motto is "No Sniveling" upgraded a decade ago from "Go Fuck Yourself" abbreviated to GFY in situations when it would be impolite to use the F word.

The Board Meetings at the South End were so contentious while I sat in on them, I recall once simply getting up from my chair and lying down on the Persian carpet in the Day Room surrounded by yelling swimmers, rowers and handball players. I covered my eyes in the presence of all and pretended I no longer existed as the debate over, I think, the use of swim aids on a Kirby Cove swim (fins, wetsuits, etc.), caused our awaiting meal to both burn and go cold. Lee Block, the preeminent promulgator of the GFY-ethos at the South End predicted I would only last six months on the board as he did. I did better than twice that but could not serve out my term. The verbal riot over the shape, color, size, storage methods, dolly construction and name of a single Zodiac ("Big Red") was the end of me. "And, oh, by the way, Bruno—they're not called fucking Zodiacs! They're fucking Rigid Inflatable Boats! Get your terminology right!"

There are three ways to combat the kind of cold you find on New Year's Day Alcatraz:

1. Gain weight (which means swim slower and spend more time in the cold).
2. Wear a wetsuit but then get an asterisk by your name: "SWIM AID."
3. Attempt to outswim the cold (i.e.: get faster.).

In the Fall of 2012, I decided that I was going to outrun it, training fifty-three days in the last two months of the year. I returned to The Best Kept Secret on the San Francisco Peninsula, the San Mateo Elks Lodge, home to a number of South Enders. One of them, Tom McGrath, I first met in the South End sauna in between his handball matches when I exclaimed, "Wow! What a great shirt!" And, Tom, without a word of introduction—I had never spoken to him before—pulled the green St. Paddy's Day South End shirt off him (sopped with sweat) and handed it to me, demonstrating that South Enders will, when asked, give you the *actual* shirt off their *actual* back. (His remains my favorite South End shirt of all time—though I have since washed it.) So I returned to the Elks pool, where there is always a lane available, though at times you may need to avert your eyes from overweight men in floral trunks dog-paddling for hours between one side of the pool and the other.

At 5:30 in the morning, however, no such men exist. In early November of 2012, it was just John and me. Early morning pool etiquette is much like urinal spacing protocol among straight men in an empty restroom. You can't swim besides each other—that's like taking the middle urinal when one on the end is occupied. Neither can you swim at the far end of the pool, which is like taking to the handicapped stall to pee in private (maybe even sitting when you pee), signifying you have something to hide.

At such times, I would be forced to swim one lane away from John, where in the green gloom of the underwater pool lights John ruined my split-times with the prop-wash of diminutive feet. My one consolation was this: if we met at the wall together, I could snap a turn faster than he could rotate the heft of that torso and then spring off the wall for a one meter/one second lead. This would only piss John off. It would be like if you hit the windshield washer fluid button at the Indianapolis Speedway (assuming you had one), just as the leader of the pack is drafting inches behind you preparing to pass. Nothing good comes of such a maneuver, but, nevertheless, I could not help myself from doing it.

My "wah-KAH!" was met with his "ker-POW!" as John dropped down into a passing gear—in fact, he pulled people over at high speed for a living—and left me behind as I studied a form better used, I thought, leaping in and out of Santa's sleigh in the dead of night Christmas Eve.

John would climb out of the pool thereafter trying hard, very hard, to be self-deprecating about his early-morning performance. He'd check his time for a mile and say, "Not bad for an old man." I was four year's John's senior and a few hundred meters behind. Maybe more.

Waking up on New Year's Day in this country when most people are just getting into a deep sleep in order to plunge into cold water is a sick feeling. Swimming Alcatraz begins in bed. In the dark. Facing the cold of the bedroom night air. The cold of bare feet on the bathroom floor. It is so nauseating that I have slept in my swim parka before the swim in preparation for it. All that good, warm, twitch-filled sleepy heat you can take with you to the kitchen for the initial caffeine injection. And then drive mummified to the club lined in fleece. What does it matter? Everyone you are about to see looks like they just spent the night at your place anyway.

The upside of swimming Alcatraz on New Year's Day is that there are plenty of places to park. The swimmer who introduced me to the South End, a friend, Brandon Chaney, would invariably whisper to me on the mornings of such swims, "PSI is building," meaning that the fear within him was causing involuntary intestinal contractions (pounds per square inch) such that he would be required to shit prior to walking down the wharf to board the boat. Inevitably, my PSI would build on such mornings, too. I have no doubt men crap their pants in war, because I have come so close to crapping my Speedo at the South End on such mornings that I am developing a shit-proof pair to take to market myself: Depend-dO's. (My PSI is building as I type this, just thinking of my PSI building on such mornings. The fear, for me, is really that bad.) I might need to go shit now.

I'm back.

The best way to swim Alcatraz in the dark and in the cold is to pretend you're not. You just have to break causal links between preparatory tasks:

- I'm just getting up early!
- I'm just accumulating food in the kitchen!
- I'm just going to go for a drive in the dark with the heat on high and Foo Fighters playing!
- I'm just going to go see some old friends!

Soon you are kissing your favored swimmers of the opposite sex with *Something About Mary* bedhead and forcing down oatmeal with peanut butter or rice milk stirred with protein powder or a Cliff Bar with a Gu chaser. Then PSI is about to blow! So upstairs quickly to the twin toilet stalls which you can tell are occupied because when you look over the stall door some scared, sleepy friend is looking up at you: "*Hi!*" Eventually, you get a stall or use the toilet in the handicapped sauna downstairs, but eventually all the fear in the shit is shat out. The fear remains. But not the fear in the shit. Because now there is no shit. Just the fear—besides that fear (mine) of shitting yourself.

Why do it?

Because if you don't, other people will have fun without you. That's why to do it.

Cold water swimming goes from the most social sport in the world (the kissing), to the loneliest (the water) to the most social (the sauna!).

The final lie: I'm just going for a boat ride with my friends!

So a hundred of us push in a mass through the front door of our club— the Dolphin swimmers are slower, generally, and not as attractive—except for those few swimmers who belong to both. We reassemble arm-in-arm and flip-flop down Fisherman's Wharf arrayed in swim parkas of different colors and nationalities (Sarah Mehl, who *swam* Bay-To-Breakers got a cool green one for a dollar at Goodwill). We pass Capurro's, where, Paul, a South Ender, keeps our drinks strong, our coffee hot and a few favored dogs unseen beneath the corner tables after a swim.

I'm just going for a boat ride with my friends!

The first omen that we were in trouble on January 1st, 2013 was that the swim instructions at the briefing were wrong. They had to be. I had never heard such a thing before in my life: fast swimmers swim to the breakwater—to the *east* of the opening to Aquatic Park. Slower swimmers focus on The Pump House to the *west*. Did I hear that right? Is that possible? For two sets of swimmers to swim to two different points of the compass? But any attempt for clarification on any swim at the South End is responded to like this, "Just swim toward land, Chris—*ha! ha! ha!*"

Unfortunately, it's always funny. *No Sniveling!* To inquire as to tidal guidance beyond a mere initial request is to snivel. You can't do that.

The harbinger that this would be a swim I might never forget is when I saw that cold, dark bay water was stirring below the stern of our boat in the harbor *before* the engine was started. It appeared to me, looking down into a liquid black mix-master at the dock, that the entire continent had its own propellers engaged and was prepared to back away from this entire event. Thus did I have a sense of foreboding before the lines were cut. We pulled away from our berth in a forty-foot tourist tender with room in the cabin for maybe a dozen people. Thirty more were on deck and we had one other such boat, and a flotilla of kayaks and Zodiacs—er, RIB's—making their way in the darkness before us—headlamps and blinking lights appearing in the distance.

The water was sloppy behind the breakwater which protected the fleet in the harbor, but when we turned at "the Creakers," a moaning stand of water-logged pilings, it was apparent we were about to be in real trouble: white-caps all the way to the island and grab-for-support swells mid-channel.

I might have shit myself for fear but for the lack of it—my intestines a boa constrictor looking for something to choke to death, chew up and spit out.

Everyone was nervous. Sometimes you get lucky out there. Other times not. This time was not. All that was left to do was to steel yourself over the course of the next thirty or forty minutes that you were here to do this work. That you were capable of it.

The lies were over: I'm going to swim this thing.

The mantra of open water swimming was penned by Tom Petty: "the waiting is the hardest part."

The waiting, Tom.

The waiting.

It is the hardest, hardest part. You await a stay of execution. That stay never comes. You are to commit yourself to an embrace of such coldness it will force the air from your lungs. You will hit the water willing your lungs to expand because they will not do it otherwise.

I made for the wheelhouse where I warmed myself before the fire of Pedro "The Push" Ordenes's unfailing Latin optimism and warmth. "Sometimes when you find yourself in the gutter," he consoled me with an accent so thick it is noticeable in both Americas, "you simply need to look up at the stars." I huddled in my swim parka—can I swim with it?—and finding an extra swim cap in one pocket, decided to put one beneath my thermal cap and one above—the only time I had ever done that before, but something that seemed like a security blanket when the security of dry land was getting farther and farther behind us as we crested each roller and slid down the other side toward as fabled an island as exists anywhere in the world.

I stood closest to a door I wanted to slide closed for the little bit of extra warmth. When the captain cut the motor, I was reminded of an Angel Island swim when a fellow South Ender, *Buddha Todd*, confessed he ran away to Alaska to fish commercially when he was fourteen. Todd reminded me that he was terrified when the engine of his purse-seiner was cut as it always meant the end of rest and the commencement of tough physical labor in all types of inclement weather. I had run away to Alaska myself at seventeen and subconsciously endured that very same terror every time a motor is cut on the water. *The work is at hand.*

I looked out that door and spied our other boat rising and dipping with the waves. There on the stern stood John Flahavan. Alone. Clad only in his Speedo and yellow South Ender swim cap. With a wind blowing in from The Gate at 11 mph for our 8:15 AM jump, the wind chill brought the temperature below forty degrees, causing what we knew would be a sub-100 degree swim (combination of air and water temperature) to be a sub-90.

John was stripped down and ready to fight. He alone stared out at our fate. I stared out at him.

Sometimes bravery is merely the will to act in spite of one's fear. But sometimes bravery is the damn-the-torpedoes type that rushes headlong into conflict with such quickness that trepidation cannot keep up. To me on that day, at that moment, John demonstrated that he was made of this tougher stuff. He would need no parka, no last-minute Gu, no wheelhouse warmth or gallows humor. He was ready to start this thing. To lead the pack. To be the first one in and across.

That pecking order of swimmers among us is not limited to just speed. The real ranking is courage. And it exhibits itself on longer swims, lonelier swims, tougher swims. My ranking, therefore, is probably lower than most, as I tend to avoid many greater solo challenges (Roundtrip Angel Island, Trans-Tahoe, etc.) in order to draft behind better swimmers on more crowded swims whose presence and conviction cause me to swim harder in their presence. So though I might say I swam a particular swim, I know in my heart I could not have finished as I had without the presence of so many people I had come to admire—John, foremost among them. Seeing John alone at the stern of that boat caused me to toughen up. I would not be the first one on deck to remove my swim parka, as John had, nor would I be the first to enter the water, but neither would I be last to do so either.

He led me at the Elks. He would lead me here. I would follow him. I would follow.

The shock of water that cold all over your body—total immersion from which you cannot escape—and the sensation of slipping beneath the surface of something which in winter can kill you activates the survival mechanism of a stroke that has yet to fail me, but the breathing never comes naturally at 49 degrees—not to me anyway. The breathing can kill you. You must control your lungs. And to do that you have to slow your pulse. What gets you to land is your breath. And you must catch it. Or terror will take hold. As I approached the stern of the boat, I was slowing my breath, relaxing myself, telling myself I needed that shock of cold. I needed it to do my work. I wanted it. There is one among us called *Reptile*. He urges us to find our inner lizard. I embraced my scaled past and made the leap.

The shock of that ice cold liquid embrace exceeds the capacity of the human body to feel. It is too great a transition. It is electric.

The thing has come.

Goggles? No leaks. No fog.

Cap? Smooth across my head.

I reach for water and begin my kick—everything now is the breathing.

That initial shakedown of limbs is merely an attempt to regulate respiration when every muscle which makes up the chest demands contraction. To succeed in cold water swimming, one must adopt a *Being John Malkovich* approach to controlling the semi-submersible vessel of your body. You must become a vicious U-Boat commander staring at the gauges in a rugged scow of limited range and resources that is trying to make its home port despite the shelling of bad weather, worse tides, chop and diminishing blood sugar levels.

The hardest thing about swimming from Alcatraz, especially with a relative small number of swimmers, is the overwhelming nothingness of the experience. To your left is miles of water. And a very tall bridge. To your right are even more miles of water and another tall bridge. Beyond it, the curvature of the Earth. The analog on land is to cut through the fence at JFK or O'Hare or SFO, march out to the end of the runway, dig a hole as deep as you are tall, jump in and, getting up on your tiptoes, put yourself at eye level to the tarmac. Now spin slowly around. Nothing. That is what it is like swimming from Alcatraz. The fastest way home is to look down. Straight down. Look into the gloom. Get streamlined.

Look at nothing. Lift your head for the smallest peek at land. If the tide is running (and, generally, it does counter to advice given you in The Briefing), you will have to adjust your angle of attack across the channel. If you remember to peek beneath your armpit (learnt from *The Push!*), you can triangulate off Alcatraz Island behind you. If you are lucky, you can find a great swimmer-navigator who you can track all the way across: Dianna Schuster, God Rest Her Soul, was the best. Look for her stroke. If you draft behind Dianna (as I did every chance I had), she becomes your sherpa, lifting her head, stopping for a moment, checking for drift, and then heads down once more to get to The Opening. My times improve behind her.

But today the waves do not permit such views. I am alone. All alone. And in seas I would not venture out in a boat. If I am aligned to The Pump House besides Fort Mason—and I am—then this simply becomes Time-Over-Target: I put in my strokes, monitor the cold in my extremities—some coolness now along the back of my hands, at my thighs and one foot, but I feel good. My greatest fear is getting so deep into my stroke and my thoughts that I forget where I am. That happens all the time. I have no idea where I am or what I am doing. I am deep in my thoughts, ignoring the tide—the stroke becomes hypnotic—and then I either discover to my horror I am terribly off-track or, as once occurred, Bob Roper, the fastest man ever to swim the Golden Gate, might perform a high-speed U-turn around in an actual Zodiac and yell, "SWIM TO MID-SPAN!"

That would be mid-span of the most photographed object on Earth. Look at a map. That is due West of any course from Alcatraz to San Francisco. To be told to:

A. Stop what you are doing,
B. Swim due West
C. In a tone which means "as fast as you can,"

demonstrates that the trouble you are in is nearly unrecoverable and that you have been given a few hundred yards to sprint before Bob Roper returns to pull you out of the water. I think it would be safe to say that no one in the history of Alcatraz swimming has ever been given that particular command but me. I swam for my life then, listening to Bobbie's return. I could smell the two-cycle exhaust as he circled. He slowed, idled down, checked the drift, and called a new command, "ROPER TOWERS!" the twin, curved condominium towers at Aquatic Park which he convinced me he either built, or now owns (thanks to shaking down fellow South Enders each winter for his Christmas fund)—this, my new vector to make The Opening on my own. I've never been pulled on fifty-plus Alcatrazes. But bragging rights begin at the South End at one hundred. I, a mere slacker.

Virtual Band-Aids precede the coming of The Claw. Numbness on your fingers which limits the ability to gauge the angle of attack of your hands at the commencement of each stroke means you are guessing as to the efficiency with which you pull yourself forward. If only the Band-Aids remain—you are probably in good shape. But The Claw, when it comes, affects the entire hand. The fingers curve inward of their own volition and then you slow despite your stroke per minute. And the virtual wetsuit which materializes on any cold water swim which prevents you from feeling cold, although you are, can disintegrate in really cold water and hypothermia can begin to take effect. You can feel it happen. I watched a good friend freeze up beside me as we swam from AT&T Park. He was deep in a trance as he swam, unresponsive to my voice, taking a slight turn toward shore, swimming to somewhere inside his head. I flagged down a kayak and saw him later on a stool in the shower, hunched over and trembling as though in a demonic possession.

I was cold on this swim, but not hypothermic. I was mid-channel now, I was sure.

I stopped to lift my head—something you don't want to do too often—and was surprised to see that I was short of mid-channel. I looked back at Alcatraz—it was much larger than it should have been. My forearms were chilled. I commenced swimming again—wanting to return to the familiarity and comfort of my stroke—and turned the helm over again to the unshaven, uncaring U-Boat Commander inside. He repeated for me advice from Reptile: "Count your strokes." When there is so much unknown in a swim, what is known is your own propulsion: just count your strokes. A hundred maybe? Two hundred? You always know how far you can swim. I chose four—four hundred strokes. That's a quarter-mile in slack water. A quarter-mile always gets you out of trouble in an open water swim and it slows your heart rate as your realize you remain in control of your own propulsion—though a chop had risen and full breaths were irregular: they had to be timed to dips in the sea where a hollow allows for it.

I counted my four hundred and then lifted my head.

"Shit!"

I had not moved. Not perceptibly. I was on course, but caught in an ebb. If I had thought I was halfway across previously, then I was probably at the twenty-five minute mark and now another ten or so, worse case, for this four hundred. I put my head down and counted out another four hundred—knowing no tide can hold me for a half mile and making sure I remained on track for The Pump House.

You can't fight the cold. You just have to outrun it and make sure a belly full of food is providing energy. I was cold enough to shiver—a rarity on a swim this short. But constant movement, a commitment to form, staring into the gloom is the fastest way to get warm.

Four hundred more strokes and I lifted my head. After performing a calculus based on my sightlines, I determined that this was not a swim I could ever finish on my own.

It was over.

I must have been approaching fifty minutes and maybe I was slightly better than halfway across. I couldn't see anyone. I couldn't see a pilot, a boat, a swimmer, a Zodiac, Bob, an RIB, someone who could tell me to go fuck myself. No one.

I was fucked. Myself.

My U-Boat commander measured fuel remaining, effort expended, the force of the tide, the effect of the cold, the coming of The Claw and realized it was time to either abandon the course, or abandon the ship. Panic would kill me before the cold could, so I decided that to stop swimming, even momentarily, and allow the effect of the cold to catch up with me as I lifted my hand for help could put me in peril worse than I found myself in at that moment—I still had my breath. And if decidedly middle-of-the-pack me was about to blow his ballast tanks and signal for the coldest, most body-numbing, wave-pounding ride home, there probably were swimmers on that morning in greater need for assistance than I was. There's an even greater risk to running an RIB back to the club with a cold swimmer—that of leaving the other swimmers alone. One of our pilots made that hard choice and returned to discover her three swimmers *gone*—swept out The Gate on a five-knot ebb, only to be picked up by fishing boats that should not have been there. *Gone.*

I could still swim. But I could not fight this tide anymore or make it to The Cove, but there was a chance I thought I could still make it to shore.

I turned in the direction I was being pushed toward the entire swim—Fort Mason or maybe beyond it, to Gas Harbor—and calculated that if I could still get across this channel, swimming with the ebb instead of against it, I would make landfall inside a deep slip built for Liberty Ships. I thought the climb out would suck at the piers, but I headed in that direction anyway, thinking to hell with this swim, to hell with open water swimming, to hell with the South End—I quit!

I would climb out on the rocks, climb up to the parking lot, smash the window of a parked car with whatever I could carry from the breakwater with unfeeling hands and huddle inside, scratching my Alexander Super-tramp epitaph on a door panel. If I am to be found dead, I want only to be found dry. That's all.

This newfound hope of embracing failure on this swim, of giving up hope of a glorious finish on the first day of the year and just settling for survival, caused me to extend my stroke, focus on my breath, ignore additional evidence of my freezing up and for first time maybe in the entire swim to really pull for a conclusion to this contest. I wasn't trying to be brave by continuing to swim. I simply thought it was the more pragmatic decision. And those many, many miles I put in with John allowed my mind to relax a bit while that muscle memory which develops from training eases into a routine that clicks off meters in a steady manner.

I was not tired. I was just cold.

To my surprise, I now could not keep on my course to Fort Mason. I was pointed back toward The Pump House—back east! Was there to be no slack water between the tides? Through the gate called golden before a bridge was even built—exactly two miles due west—pumped three hundred and ninety *billion* gallons of salt water between high and low tides. *Three hundred and ninety billion.*

Peter Gabriel has a song for it: *Here Comes The Flood!*

I was lifted up out of the water by a force which could allow a seal to swim up a wave and stand like Jesus at its crest on just his hind flipper. I came down in a trough too deep to swim out of. When I looked up, one of The Dolphin's varnished vintage rowboats—the Joe Bruno?—rose above and before me—two rowers: a woman and man, their oars pointed straight down. I could see the blades.

"GO TO THE OPENING!" the woman cried, holding one arm east.

"NO!" I said. I had given up.

The pair fell into a trough as I rose to the height of their bow.

"GO TO THE OPENING!" she cried again, rising once more, as I fell below her.

"NO!" I said. No more making for home, I had decided. Then a thought. "FARNSWORTH!" I cried. I will go through the barnacle-en-crusted Farnsworth Gap *through* The Muni Pier—that would cut the route in half!

"GO TO THE OPENING!" She insisted.

And then I was hit by the locomotive of a current headed toward Oakland—a river of water close to shore that would overcome the propulsion of anything or anyone caught within it.

From that spot in between the Muni Pier and the Pump House and until I reached the opening to Aquatic Park, across the entire length of the Muni Pier, I did not take a single stroke. I rolled on my back to prevent the whiplash of being sent headfirst into a trough and brought my arms into my chest, kicking to stay current with the crest I rode so that I would not fall below it again. And I thought of Pedro's prophetic advice to me on the boat: "When you find yourself in the gutter, sometimes you just need to look at the stars."

And when that prophecy of his hit me, I realized that my swim was over—that with something like a half mile still to travel, no more effort would henceforth be required. I was done. I relaxed in a cradle of warmth, in the arms of safety with the crumbling goodness of the beautiful reinforced concrete Muni Pier that I could just reach out and kiss, feeling its crags with my lips—my home upon the water, this fortress in the cold, a pre-historic water-logged Stonehenge emerging from the depths, the most beautifully wretched structure on this Earth. I glided by it with ease, wishing for this water slide never to end. I rolled over on my stomach at the turn and, as though I was stepping off a merry-go-round as it slows, picked my path toward our sandy beach, placing one arm before the other, breathing easily and taking my place in the wagon-train of yellow-capped swimmers who had found a path across what could only be called troubled waters on that morning. An easy quarter mile of calm water passed by in The Cove as I glided by the three-masted schooner, Balclutha. Our journey ended at the two outstretched piers of both clubs—outstretched like arms: we swam up between them until our fingertips touched sand.

We then arose on our legs and walked out.

Irish Coffees are served on the beach at the South End just one block from where they had been introduced in this nation, but I went right for the club house, so cold was I. Paul Springer expressed surprise that I had not been pulled—I don't know whether he had. I couldn't reply as I stepped into plastic basin of fresh water used to dissolve the accumulated sand, our ceremonial cleansing of our feet, effectively, before entering the club. I scampered through the lower Boat House to the Upper and took my turn on the wooden stairs up to our locker room—stairs that paint cannot stick to at the treads because they are so often, as now, sodden.

As a former hypothermic, I fear the sauna this cold. The last warm blood I had, I knew, was circulating at my brain and my heart. I was in for an hour at least. Heat up the skin too quickly and the cold blood circulates too fast—next stop Konxville. That's Konxville. Not Knoxville. Instead, I turned on what I thought was tepid water in the shower and stayed underneath it until the coldness really began, until I shivered, until I shook with a manic palsy so severe I am eyed by my fellow South

Enders trying themselves to recover. Shivering, though, is good in such circumstances—it means your body is able to begin to register the cold. Blood is beginning to flow. In increments I could sense how warm the water was that was falling upon me (we argue about the shower heads at the South End, the water flow at the South End and the water temperature at the South End). With care I increased the temperature, retrieving a stool from the locker room to ensure I am closer to the ground if I am to fall upon it. In time, I can feel the heat of the water equally all over my body—then, and only then, can I enter the sauna.

Gary Emich among all the others awaited me. All were naked, exposing the greatest variance of skin tone color imaginable: greys, reds, pinks, white. We all thaw of our own accord, numbers Sharpied on our triceps, the warmest among us talking the most and shaving with elegance on a little bit of Dr. Bronner's Peppermint liquid soap to make the razor glide. Evidently, Gary saw a look on my face that warm water can never thaw. "That was one of the roughest Alcatrazes of my life," he said. Coming from Gary that meant something—he and Stevie Ray Hurwitz have swum over a *thousand* of them.

John Flahavan passed me in the locker room as I dressed. I was still cold. "Good one," he said.

"Good one, John?" I thought. "Good one?"

Quitting appealed to me. Really quitting. Quitting everything. Quitting the South End. What was the point?

I threw away my card key. Didn't pay my locker dues and allowed the voracious maw of the South End Lost & Found to digest my beloved swim parka, my black Speedo with SOUTH END embroidered on the ass and my array of ointment and lotions and wax ear plugs and brass scraps, which I, like other South Enders, salvaged from Southender Beach, as we called it, on the North end of Alcatraz. It was as illegal for us to land on Alcatraz as it was to take stuff with us that we found buried in the sand. I abandoned it all.

Who needs it?

Go. Fuck. Yourself.

I still have the Elks. Where personal interaction is always a lesson in civility. Where you can knock on a secret panel in the locker room, which slides open, and my own personal bartender, Larry, slides across a cold can of Guinness to take to the Jacuzzi. A Jacuzzi is a machine that smashes hydrogen molecules. The friction from the smashing heats water and causes it to bubble. You can sit in it. And drink beer with fat men in floral trunks who hate swimming as much as you do. Yes, there might be South Enders I might run into at The Elks, but the only one I dreaded to see was John.

I actually practiced lines I would say to him when we would next hold doors open for the other at The Elks. I practiced them out loud to defend my decision to quit. Such is the respect—maybe even fear—a slow swimmer has for a fast one. A really fast and determined one like John.

Then I heard the news he was dead.

It hit me like the wave that snuck up behind me swimming a rollicking Sundowner Gas-House Nose-Ring Pauly organized one Friday Night for The Underachievers when I was thrown down into a trough with such force my legs were bent around so they touched my back and I emerged without a swim cap. I could not breathe.

John Flahavan? Dead?

His funeral Mass was held in a church and a city which bears the name of the first ship to enter the San Francisco Bay. And the first ship to leave it. San Carlos.

Appropriate for John was was first in and first out of all our swims. Finishing thus lends itself to a solitary existence at the South End because the greatest comfort after such great contests is the brotherhood that can only be found during the slow, very slow, exceedingly slow warm-up in winter in the sauna that could easily amount to more time than the swim itself. It is the smallest, most elect and intimate gathering of men that I have ever known, and owing to John normally finishing first, I never spent enough time with him in the sauna to so much as to get to know him.

*   *   *

"CLOSE THE DOOR!" is a familiar cry in the South End sauna. Not just because as your core body temperature rises to normal you become hyper-sensitive to minute changes in ambient temperature—*don't let the cold air in!*—but because fucking El Sharko is lurking—his dorsal fin cutting through the kindness of the locker room in silence. El Sharko, who conquered The English Channel and swam from Alcatraz once with a brass valve the size and weight of a cantaloupe—he will rush us with the garden hose from the shower once we are toasty and *blast* us with a freshwater stream as cold as the bay in winter. *"CLOSE THE DOOR!"*

John's death whispered to me just the opposite: "Open the door, Chris. Open it."

Home is where you are loved. Not where your heart is. But where the hearts exist which love you. Sometimes you don't have control of where you are loved, why it occurs or who does the loving. But home is where you are loved. And as I am loved more at the South End than any other place else on Earth, I returned.

"You don't join the South End," says Andy Fields, who did not live long enough to see these words in print. "It joins you."

The South End joined me. And John did, too.

And if I feared John Flahavan's reproach more than anyone else's at my leave-taking, I realize he would be most satisfied (probably not happy, but satisfied) at my return.

Sheepishly, lacking some of the bravado for which previously both John and I were known, I made my way back.

On the warmest, fastest and most calm St. Francis Yacht Harbor swim of my life, when I matched Carol Merryfield stroke-by-stroke—I read of her Alcatraz ambitions in SWIMMER magazine and found her on Linked In before The Dolphins could lay a greasy fin on her—we emerged like the dancers in Vonnegut's *Harrison Bergeron*—feeling so superhuman by our speed and our grace in calm water that we should have had chains to hold us back. We emerged in sunlight to the smiles and laughter of South Ender's finishing up a row, preparing for another one, washing out an RIB and congregating on the small deck behind our club.

Bill Wygant, then president of the South End Rowing Club met us there, when there was no rush for the shower or the recuperative effects of the sauna and said, apropos of nothing, "All you have to do to swim in open water is to get over your fear of death."

That's a direct quote.

I'm more likely to get eschatological on the club's Google Groups email list than Bill (me or Johhny Diesel, that is), but it was he who was existential on a brilliant warm fall day when global warming seemed like the most pleasant way to meet the *Waterworld* of our impending doom. Death was the farthest thought on my mind.

But he's right in a way.

Though I will never get over that fear.

Ever.

Can't shit that one out.

I will never get over it.

I do have a way of understanding it though. Because of the South End. Because of John and all the people there.

Death is a swim I have signed up for that I hope will never come. I hope it never does. But when I awake in the dark to be ferried to the point where I am to drop on deck the swim parka of my flesh, to leave behind its warmth and familiarity and commit myself to the unknown, I know I will be alone again, and cold again, and scared again, but I will hope that I will have done all in my life to prepare myself for that final crossing in order to track a true course home, to steady emotions gone frantic, and to emulate the courage of those who have gone before me.

It is not eternity I will hope for when I make that jump, or for some great expanse, or a multitude from the ages. As I struggle to get to the other side then, I will hope only for the reward that is mine when I swim: one small place to receive me, a warm room where plum-favored potcheen has been smuggled from Derry on my behalf, where Joe Butler's oatmeal growler is passed from lips, to lips, to lips. Where Tim Spicer is not just a name on a RIB, and Johnny da Brewer and his moviestar good looks await our next game of aquatic tennis ball tag. A place of understanding and laughter, and endeavor, where I am loved, and where I will see John Flahavan again and where I can say in his presence not "an ad-libbed line well-rehearsed," but the thing that is always on my mind at such times, but I was never courageous enough before to say to him in person, "Thank God we made it, John."

Thank God.

poem

Falling for Gravity

joanell serra

(1)

on the day that gravity broke
kindergarteners laughed
waving their arms like blue birds
reaching for their swimming goldfish crackers

an older boy – almost twelve –
recognized the Icarusonian nature
of their choice
tossed jump-rope lassos to the sky

an east village physics professor
the first to grasp the new order
soaked his shoes in freshly poured cement
and strode down Houston Street

the neighborhood drug dealer
yelled down for help
haloed
by tiny bags of white powder

> the structures we relied upon-
> suspension bridges
> the tides
> the weight of oppression
> the thrill of roller coasters
> all rendered meaningless

(2)
people have learned to hold on
to visit one another
swinging through the canopies
of oak trees in central park

belaying from apartment balconies,
rooftop gardens
and theatre signs on 42ncd Street
 clipped to decaying telephone lines

occasionally someone departs
from despair
or perhaps accidentally
letting go long enough to cover a cough

we stop to watch
rocks tied to our waists
tears floating up
hearts heavy, while limbs grow lighter

in a true reversal
pregnant women have it easier
they move like ballet dancers
down the grocery store aisles

as if we're all meant
to carry another person inside us
to tether ourselves
to the next generation

to strike
the perfect balance
of blood and bone
love and liquid

fiction

The Floor Noise Management Center
nina schuyler

So we figured we'd set up some sort of system for the complaints piling up like Mount Hallasan among apartment dwellers, and see… well, it seemed like a good idea at the time for people to call and rant, blow off some steam about their neighbors' noises. And the goal, see, was to de-escalate things and avoid things getting out of hand. With so many people working from home these days, we had to do something because, like I said, the complaints were stacking up. It was going all right, for the most part, but then I got a call from the parents of a young boy who said their neighbor, in revenge for their son running back and forth—he was only five—was blasting Buddhist chants.

I had talked to the young son's parents earlier, and they'd been contrite and said they wouldn't let it happen again, but I guess it didn't work. So I called the man blasting the chants and asked gently, didn't he remember being a small boy with loads of energy? He said he didn't. He was a good boy, obedient and disciplined, and did what his parents told him to do. I also said in the nicest possible way that the chants were meant, you know, to create harmony, and he was, well, sort of misusing them. He told me to call his neighbors and tell them to buy their son a pair of slippers or tether him to his bedpost.

I was going to call the parents again but got sidetracked by a call from an angry woman who said her neighbor was singing La Traviata, starting at 7:00 am. I might have put up with it, she said, but he had an enormous, tuneless voice like an injured animal stuck under a truck tire. I speculated maybe he was trying to become an opera singer and needed to practice. Fine, she said, but make him practice in the park, far away from her apartment. I said I'd see what I could do, so I called the aspiring opera singer, and he told me he loved the opera ever since he was a boy. He knew he wasn't very good, but he was fifty-two years old and wasn't getting any younger—if not now, when? I could empathize; I was fifty and this was the only job I could get, though at the end of the day, my head felt as if it were webbed with smoldering wires. When I suggested the park, he said people in the park always told him to go home and practice. Besides, the crows kept circling him and cawing loudly, and he found it hard to concentrate. By the way, said the man, the woman who complained about him? She was getting her revenge by having loud sex. Moaning and groaning, and when she climaxed, she screamed at the top of her lungs, and her bed frame repeatedly hit his wall.

Well, I said, not sure what to say. I looked at the script our boss handed us to use if we got tongue-tied. You'll have to work it out, I said. Fat chance, he said.

We expected complaints about shouting couples and blaring TVs, vacuum cleaners and front doors slamming, tea kettles hissing and shrieking, the opening and closing of kitchen cabinets, children running, skipping, laughing, squealing, giggling, yelling, sobbing, newborns crying, and dogs barking. We anticipated retaliation—earsplitting music, yelling matches, vacuum cleaners thundering at 11:00 pm, and blenders bellowing at 5:00 am.

So I didn't expect a call about a man playing golf in his apartment. The woman said the golfer played eight, ten hours a day, the ball rolling above her head. It was like listening to a dripping faucet. Occasionally, her neighbor took a full swing, and the ball smacked the wall, causing the woman to jump, her apartment to shake, the pictures on her wall to rattle, and sometimes fall. The golfer said he'd lost his job and was so bored if he didn't play golf, he'd have to play baseball, and he thought whacking the ball and slamming it into a handmade net would be louder. Besides, said the golfer, the woman who called to complain was drilling holes in the wall to get back at him. Twenty-seven so far. Well, see, I was going to call the driller back when I noticed my phone's red light was blinking, and I had 752 messages waiting, so I told the golfer to try to work it out.

For the next few days, I dealt with complaints about rowdy parties; a loud piano, trumpet, oboe, violin, and cello playing; a vigorous ping pong game; skateboarding with a half-pipe; a parrot that squawked, How are you? and What the hell; and a woman who kept breaking glasses.

Then I got the call from a man who said his neighbor was revving a jet motor in his apartment. He had to listen to the revving all day, sometimes roaring up to what sounded like 200 miles per hour. The noise was splitting open his skull, and he didn't know how much more he could take. Imagine your head stuck under the hood of a car, someone pressing down on the gas pedal, but stuck in neutral. The jet motor builder was somewhat apologetic. Of course he was, he knew it was loud, but Seoul Air Mechanics, where he usually tested engines, was closed for at least a month. Well, you know, I have to say I sympathized. I'd always been fascinated by engines of all types, and he had a job to do. So, I called his neighbor back and explained the jet engine builder's predicament. He said if the engine builder continued gunning his engine, he'd have to shoot him.

I chuckled but later told my colleagues I regretted this response and maybe I could have done more because he did, in fact, shoot the jet engine builder. Someone who lived on the other side of the engine builder noticed the quiet and called me. He knew we only dealt with noise, but maybe we could make an exception and deal with an eerie silence. I called the police, and they found the man dead on his living room floor, the engine beside him, tables overturned, lamps smashed, and fingerprints of his irate neighbor on his neck.

In the office, we solemnly gathered in the conference room, all of us rattled by this turn of events. My wife and young son came to the office to console me. We shook our heads and drank tea, and in the background, we could hear the phones' incessant ring.

My son asked, Can mankind ever get along? I said, I don't know. Can the self ever be transcended so one can think of the greater whole? he said. I said, Given what I listen to day in and day out, I have my doubts. My colleagues nodded sadly. How will civilization ever endure then? said my son.

I didn't know what to say and felt a sorrow welling up in me, taking all the moisture from my mouth.

I don't like this, he said.

We stood together and slowly became aware of a silence, not an everyday silence of desolation, but a pure silence that resided underneath the noise. It was a silence that ran like a clear, unpolluted river under the racket and calamity of humanity. It had been there always and would always be there. The quality of light changed and became softer, and all the faces in the room were beautiful. In that moment, it was as if none of the phones were ringing, and the world had drifted into a peaceful existence.

The ringing phone jarred me out of my glorious daydream, and now the noises rose all around me. I picked up the receiver. A donkey, yelled a woman, in the apartment above her, a deafening hee-haw.

Vigilance

morgan reed

I knew it was weird
to wake up as my neighbor
in her ridiculous pajamas,
peeking through the blinds at 2 AM.
But once in her skin, I couldn't help being curious
about a light that was burning
in what might have been a dungeon
in my own house.

Meanwhile, her security lights flipped on,
giving the brazen raccoons in back
a clearer view for their work
of digging up the vegetable garden.

It wasn't my fault.
I can't answer
for anything, since I was surely on Safari
at the time. Somewhere, a server
knows, and remembers. Must I explain,
in this still-free country?

She probably won't be happy
tomorrow, when she wakes up
as herself and wonders
exactly which part of her life
went missing
during the night.
How can we keep order
when those we can't even see
come uninvited and undercover
to steal from us?

Sepia and Saffron

jamie grove

Outside, the air is thick and the sky has taken on a doomsday glow. It's all a yellow fog and a red sun. Overnight almost, the fire smoke blew in and settled heavy in town like a blanket.

I put my things down. Even inside the house, the smell of smoke lingers, and it looks hazy and dark. It's almost been a full ten years since I've been back, and mostly the house seems the same, but I have to take a moment to adjust. I open the blinds for what little light will filter in, light a candle, do the settling in things I would if I were in my own home.

I say hello to Mom, but she's silent. She's looking at me, but I can't make eye contact. There's a hitch in my throat, maybe from the smoke, maybe the emotion.

I turn on the news, which is still reporting the same old thing about weather and temperature and wind gusts. I'm seldom not listening to the news these days. It's always on, so it's become a drone in the background, a buzz at the back of my skull. Occasionally, the anchors change it up by talking about the rumors flying around about leftist crazies with chainsaws and gas cans, setting fires in the night. Roaming herds of anarchists, like out of some movie. The anchors give little breath to the lightning storms and droughts and ever climbing temperatures. You have to listen to public radio for that, not network TV.

There's a musk to the house that can't be explained by the fire smoke. It's the smell of dust and old cigarettes, yesterday's bacon grease still in the pan. I wish I could open the windows to let in the fresh air, but there's nothing fresh about the air anymore. Just the smoke and gloom.

Without something better to do, I start wiping things down. I can't keep the grit and ash off the things in the house any more than I can keep it from creeping in through the cracks. I can feel it with every exhale, gathering all over the house and mingling with all the usual household odors and must. But it's still something I can do, an easy thing to tackle and obsess over, so I start dusting and wiping and wringing out the mud in the sink.

While I'm working, I keep catching glimpses of Mom out of the corner of my eye. For now she's at the dinner table, looking tired, her full, heavy belly rising and falling against the table's edge with every echo of a breath.

She might be dozing. She looks like she's gathering herself, pulling herself, literally, together. I'm afraid to look right at her, like she's a mirage that would disappear. Still, I can tell the circles are dark beneath her eyes. There are hollows where her cheeks should be. She's as yellow as the sky.

I work around the table carefully, making a space for myself at it, but all my wiping only drives the grit deeper into the table's crevices. So much ash in the house just overnight. So much dust from before. There's a subtle difference between the heft of dush and ash. A tiny deviance in grain and weight between the two. Years of dinners and homework and check writing has left the table scratched and scarred, looking a little worse for the wear. Mom and the table make a matching set.

"Long drive?" Mom finally says.

She wants to talk, now that I can't be ignored anymore. Or maybe it's just that she's gathered enough of herself that she can manage it.

"Not too bad," I reply. "There's not too many people out driving today, probably staying inside. The air's almost toxic out there."

I laugh because for some reason this strikes me as funny, and the sound echoes a little in the empty kitchen.

I can't shake the feeling that I brought the fire with me. It's stupid; it's giving myself a bigger role in the world than I have any right to. Still, I got the call about Mom that meant I had to come down right away, and the fire came too. It's stupid, I know it's stupid, but I still can't shake it. The fire started the day I drove in, and by the next morning we were socked in with smoke and haze. Ash was falling from the sky. The fire was too far up the canyon to see, but I could smell it, taste it, feel it along my skin. It was close enough to merit an evacuation notice–not to leave, but to get ready. But I had just gotten there and what to take along? In the lifetime of an entire house, how do you decide what stays and what goes?

Mom's still at the table, opposite where I've been sitting for the last little while. I like it there in front of the glass door that looks out toward a plateau that drops over the river. Not that I can see much. It's away from the TV in the next room, away from the constant white noise that no matter how much I don't want to listen to anymore, I can't turn it off. I listen to the anchors bicker about lightning or arson, about weather patterns and wind speed. About how the fire makes its own wind. I don't want to listen, but I can't not listen either. So I leave it on while I sit at the table, the rickety, creaky old table. The screws have worked themselves loose from the brass legs, swept up over the years into dustpans. The brass squeaks against brass, against the glass top of it, against the dinged and scratched wooden frame.

I'm working on a list of Mom's things, the things that matter according to me. Her Le Creuset pots and pans that she swore by. The tiny stuffed bunny with one eye that she's kept her entire life and wanted to be cremated with. It's still here, and I guess that's on me. But Mom wasn't a keeper of things, not of the sentimental sort. There's a photo album, the urn with my Dad in it. There are some antique things that belonged more to him than her, like the old reel and the bamboo rod that gathered dust in the umbrella stand, even though we never owned an umbrella.

I'm overwhelmed, so I make a trip down to the store, not because I need anything really, but because I need to not be in the house. I buy things I don't need and drive over to the school, where seemingly overnight an evacuation camp has popped up like mushrooms. Tents everywhere, oranges and yellows and greens and rain flies flapping in the wind. The smoke has sunk in down here too, cloaking the field. It reminds me of foggy winter days rolling snow into snowmen—if my childhood had been yellow and vaguely apocalyptic. I drive to the bridge, which seems to be floating in it, disembodied from either bank of the river, a bridge to nowhere. A bridge floating in a muck of sepia and saffron.

I sit at the bank and pick apart a turkey sandwich under an alder. Amazingly, rafts are still floating lazily by, shooting the rapids, carrying families of tourists downstream. They–the tourists–are still out enjoying their summer vacations despite the soot layering our lungs, despite the constant air quality alerts lighting up our phones. Some of them turn and wave to me as they go by, one aims his water gun in my general direction. It falls far short, scattering ripples in the current. I throw bits of crust into the water.

Above me, a lone heron flaps, flying parallel to the river. She is lazy too, her wings cutting through the air slowly, up and down, until she finally fades into the gloom above.

Except for the rush of the river, there is an eerie, foreboding quiet. Maybe, I think, we'll never see the sky again, blue and bright and fluffy with clouds. It's all just the one cloud now.

When I get back, Mom is bumping around the back bedroom. There are drawers opening and shutting and I wonder if she's searching for something. Maybe that bunny. My things are still packed up in a duffle bag on the floor of my childhood bedroom, which is mostly unchanged from how I left it. It hardly seems worth unpacking at all. There's still a pretty good chance that I could be evacuated long before I get the chance to finish cleaning up the house.

"Get what you needed?"

The noise has stopped and here's Mom, settling into her chair, lowering herself gingerly like it might hurt if she drops too fast. I still can't look right at her, instead I look just off to the right of her. Whether I'm really seeing her, or my brain is filling in the pieces is anyone's guess. Her hair is up in a ponytail, a hairstyle she seldom ever wore, worn only on the hottest of days.

"Yeah, and then some." I toss down a bag of peach rings and chocolate raisins on the table, a bag of jerky. Comfort food.

I see where she's rifled through things in the living room, removing books from the shelves and leaving them in piles on the floor. Her old sewing box is tipped over and spilling across the carpet. The picture frames are all crooked again.

Each time I get things straightened, every time I move to another room, Mom tears the place apart again, like she's a toddler looking for something. Take the things out and move them around but don't bother putting them back again. I take a breath to keep from groaning. I'll make no headway getting things done.

I hear the newscaster say that the plume has reached New York, that the haze has settled high above the city. That smoke can travel so far baffles me. Look at all the places, all the people it crossed over. Picknickers and campers. Kids at baseball games and parks, weddings, and birthday parties, all the places where life is still happening. I've forgotten that already—that it's still normal everywhere else.

I know I can't live off junk food, that it'll make me cranky and headachy before too long, so I chop things for soup and listen to the hum of the newscast.

There's a knock—three raps—at the front door. I'm not expecting anyone and certainly not at that door. It was the door that the UPS guy left packages at, the door I slipped in when I got off the school bus because it was closer to the highway. But for the most part, the family never used it, preferring the back door instead.

Mom's neighbor Paul stands on the porch with a batch of cinnamon rolls held out in front of him like an offering. I smile and I'm not so surprised after all. It's what he always brought for everything. Cinnamon rolls as a reward for feeding his dog and watering the garden when he was gone on one of his long vacations. Cinnamon rolls when I graduated high school. For Christmas, tucked between the chocolate-covered pretzels and cookies and peanut brittle. Paul shows love with food.

"We heard. We are so sorry."

I lead Paul and the rolls through the living room over to the dining table. Mom has disappeared again, and the only sounds are the occasional burble of soup from the stove and the sound of the AC unit kicking itself on.

"Thanks, Paul. Coffee?" I start making the pot before he answers. I don't like having my nerves laid bare before people, so I keep myself busy fiddling with the machine, buying just an extra moment of time to compose myself with. It doesn't help either that Paul makes me feel small, like a kid again. My middle-aged neighbor who lived in the big white house alone with my science teacher. I change the subject. I hope we can just small talk and not talk about Mom at all.

"Do you guys have a plan? For if they up the evacuation level?"

Paul sighs and clears his throat. "Depends. Seems silly to pack up and head half a mile down the road to the evacuation camp, doesn't it? I think we'll head toward Bend and call it a vacation. But you know, the winds change all the time."

I set the coffee between us but there's no milk in the house, just a bit of sugar.

"What about you? Awful timing. First your mom, and now the fire."

"It sounds terrible, but I guess I wouldn't mind if the house went up in flames. I don't know where to start with anything." I gesture around the house.

Paul reaches across the table and pats my hand. "It's a hard thing. When Dylan's father passed, we paid for a storage unit for years, until Dylan could finally just let it go. Your mother didn't even tell us anything was wrong."

Paul looks at me over the top of his mug. He seems out of place at the table, all at once too big and too quiet. I wonder if he's ever stepped foot inside the house before. I can't remember. It seems weird suddenly that he and Dylan lived next door all this time and probably never came over. And that Mom and I never went over there.

"Mom was private like that. She didn't say anything to me until she couldn't avoid it anymore." The whole truth was that Mom had waited until she landed her in a hospital with six quarts of fluid leaking out through a tube. "She didn't want anyone feeling sorry for her."

Paul nods, knowingly. "People hate to feel pitied, but pity usually has nothing to do with it. Other people just want to be there, in whatever manner that means the most."

"I didn't realize you were so close." I'd never thought of him as much more than the cheery neighbor putting around his garden, pulling weeds, pointing out the birds nesting in the spring. Always a smile and a wave, a conversation if he could pin you to it.

"Well, maybe not. Your mother was something else, that's for sure, but we were neighbors for almost thirty years. There's a lot of history over that fence line. You know, she was the first person we met when we moved here?" Paul smiles a bit out of the corner of his mouth. "I still remember, she was wearing blue jeans and a tee shirt and it was nearly one hundred degrees outside. You were just a little thing, always hiding behind her. You never said a word until you got into Dylan's class and learned we weren't going to bite."

"I had no idea." I felt the subtle shift of reality, memories reorganizing themselves around new information. Mom had always talked about when she moved here with my dad, following him from a state park halfway across the country. She had talked about the first person she met, a burly railroader down at the store that was more bark than bite and always took his tea with sugar. But that was her story, and this was theirs.

"Oh, yeah. We were all just kids back then. We moved down from Seattle so Dylan could take his teaching job here. We didn't expect to stay long, just a few years to get some experience under his belt. But there we were, unpacking the moving truck, and there was your mother, out in the driveway with a rusty weedwhacker, trying to cut down the salsify that had cropped up."

"Salsify?" I crack the screen door a bit, only because it's getting hot inside with the stove going, but it lets the smoke in. I had almost forgotten there was still a fire coming at us.

"Those giant dandelions the size of your fist. They're called western salsify." Paul laughs. "That's what I get for being married to a high school science teacher, I can name all the plants." He doesn't seem bothered by the smoke or the heat. "I went through a foraging stage once and tried making soup out of it. Tastes about as good as it looks."

There's a crash from the bedroom, so I excuse myself to go look, thinking it's Mom but it's only the old stack of National Geographic that's slumped over on itself. That's one thing at least I know I could part with easily enough, to slough them off when Mom isn't looking. The rest of the room is a mess. All of Mom's things that need sorted and decided on. They were special to her, so now they seem special to me by proxy. I don't really care for the macrame she made in college, or the old ratty stuffed animals she'd kept since she was six, but there's a sinking feeling, something like guilt or shame, when I think about getting rid of them. To get rid of them would be to get rid of her. There's a pang too for the magazines that I paged through endlessly as a child, marveling at the bright photos of faraway places, but who wants thirty-year-old magazines? I don't have room for the things myself, in my studio apartment in the city. I have enough of my own things cluttering up the place, but all the boxes I brought for packing up her things for donating are still empty.

Paul's at the stove, stirring my soup when I come back into the room. He smiles, sheepish. "Couldn't help myself–soups need stirring. But I didn't add anything. I refrained."

"Thanks." I'm reminded of the time when Mom had been working over a pot of soup for most of the day and had popped out of the house for something. We sat down later to the most awful split pea and ham. While Mom was out, Dad had added a dash or two of cinnamon. Thought it needed something, was all he said.

I gather up the papers and forms that have spread over the table since I got there. "Don't know why I thought soup was a good idea." Except that I do know. It's gray and grim outside despite the heat. Even though it's a hot day in early September, I want soup. I want comfort. I check my phone.

Paul sits back down, the table creaking when he puts his weight on it. He glances at the phone, which I set down. "Sorry. I keep checking my phone to see if they've upped the evac notices. Bad habit."

"It's alright, I'm intruding. I was just going to bring you some goodies, and here I've made myself at home." He makes to get up but I wave him down, maybe a bit more frantically than I mean to.

"Please stay. I could use the company right now." I sigh and sit down with him. "You know how I said she didn't tell me until she really had to? We haven't talked in I don't know how long. Just a text on Christmas or here and there."

Paul nods, but his face is carefully blank. "Is that right?"

"Unfortunately."

I sneeze, three times in quick succession while Paul mulls this over. I'm always sneezing now. Sneezing up all the incinerated bits of sagebrush and scrub grass, of juniper crowns, and, further up the mountain, the acres and acres of Douglas fir. Like sneezing up funerary ashes.

Paul says nothing, not even a bless you.

The soup lid clatters off the pot, banging down to the floor. It's an awful sound that makes us both jump. I turn my head too quickly to look and Mom flitters out of view. "You didn't have to throw that," I mutter.

"What in the world?"

I wipe the lid off before putting it back up on the pot, and somewhere in the house another door slams. I look to Paul.

"Sorry. I think she's haunting the place."

Paul does not get up and leave the house. He doesn't leap from the chair and make a run for it as I expect he might. He just nods as his brow creases further, nods again like all this is normal. He pats my hand like a grandfather might. "I'd say so."

Outside, the sky has taken a decidedly more orange cast to it, a jack-o'-lantern glow. It's hot, much hotter than it has any right to be. The smoke laying low in the streets brings to mind a cool misty morning. The strange haze of it could be mistaken for a streetlamp in a snowstorm. But it's stupidly, miserably hot, hair sticking to the back of your neck hot. Everything is sticky.

"Any advice for when your mother is haunting the house you're trying to clean up to sell?"

"Not off the top of my head, no. Don't have much experience with ghosts—what's that they say, though? Unfinished business. She have much of that?"

I laugh. "A bit. An entire house full of things she didn't bother with. There's no will for any of it. It's all my problem now. Had she told me before, when she was sick, we could have sorted this all out. Now I'm stuck making copies of death certificates and trying to convince the both of us to move along."

I cringe to the sound of something else crashing. "She wasn't this loud before," I sigh. I've resigned myself to this ghost business. "Mostly I just puttered around the house talking to her while I cleaned."

"Like I said, I'm no expert on ghosts. But I suppose it's not so different from what you would do with the living. Do what you have to." Paul's voice lowers, a little above a whisper. "Are you selling the house? Is she upset about that?"

I chew on his question for a minute and the answer settles like a stone. "I think she's trying to keep me here. I can't leave if I'm still cleaning."

Paul sits back and takes a long drink of his coffee, long since gone lukewarm. There's the sound of another crash. The table shakes and Paul hesitates a moment before setting down the mug.

Such is life for the next few days. Paul comes with treats, and we chat at the old beaten-up table. I clean up after Mom, picking up things, sometimes making a dash to the garbage bin, sometimes a donation box stashed in the back of my car. Mom and I make small talk, neither of us talking about the things crashing or disappearing. Paul is game about Mom's antics and even takes to saying hello whenever he comes inside. I make little headways and begin to look forward to Paul's visits. Even for a moment, I forget about the fire.

Then, when the smoke is especially thick, our phones light up with alerts and not long after that, the knock at the door. The fire's crept on us enough that it's time for us to go. Paul goes home, presumably to grab the things that they haven't already loaded into the car. I grab my bag, still unpacked.

"Mom?" I call through the empty house. There's nothing. Nothing. Not a crash, not the rasp of her whisper in my ear. "Mom, we've got to go." But it's pointless talking to her ghost now, and I throw my things into my own car. Through the smoke, I think I can just make out the flicker of low flames in the scrub along the basalt crop. Small, sinister flickers of orange beneath the sage.

I shut the door and hesitate for a moment. If I lock the door, will Mom be able to leave? If I leave the door unlocked, what's the worst that can happen?

I head to the evacuation camp, where there's dozens of families camped out, all in identical blue and orange tents, all swept off store shelves at once. There's sleeping rolls and blankets piled up and no one bothers to take my name. I'm anonymous in the town I grew up in, in this temporary community staffed by volunteers and Samaritans who chase fires around so they can do good.

A few days later, the wind shifts, the fire follows, and we're all allowed to go home. As fast as it's rolled in, the smoke is gone again.

I open the door to an empty house and know immediately Mom's gone.

I set to the work the best I know how.

When the Dead Visit

t. clear

They don't want that glass of wine,
though you offer anyway, the good host.
It'd run right through their less-than-bodies —
a last wisp of water in a drying stream.
But a chair? Sure.

Listen: forget regrets. Forget everything
you wish you'd said or done
because the dead only want
to hover, your presence
like a last steak dinner, missed.
Cannibal? —no. Inevitable
that we're all reduced to cellular breakdown
at the last, a softening of connective tissues.

So what is it you want to say?
(Addressed, of course, to both the dead and you.)
Listen, now.
Wait for it.

Is it welcome? Is it good-bye?
Is it the lifting of a thousand starlings
rising at once from the emptied field,
tipped out of song, a wingbeat-rush,
a muffle? —nothing
to decipher what you just heard,
anything it was,
it wasn't.

nonfiction

God, Goldilocks, Growing Up
tanya ruckstuhl

I was in a bad marriage with a good man. He was an atheist. I joined a cult. It stirred up some shit.

"Why do they invite us to a volunteer appreciation dinner and then hit us up for more donations?" he asked. "I'm not gonna donate when I'm already volunteering."

I was the one volunteering.

There was a long list of things he wouldn't do. Wake up early, or go to church, or donate money, or volunteer time. But I could do those things on my own.

It would be years before I understood our secret pact: he got to be a man of leisure, while I hid from my resentment of this by staying busy. I was young and dumb, lacking all self-protective skepticism, easily wooed by a tall, sophisticated man, giddy over his finely honed ability to explain things and missing entirely his inability to actually do anything.

Then our twins were born and our love for them completely eclipsed our love for each other. Children are such unfair competition. The babies were a sunny day in the bleakest winter, while we were each stale bread crusts in a compost bin of rotting food. At bedtime, he sang to the boys in high Elvish while reading them Tolkien. I took baby sign language classes so they could communicate before their vocal cords developed. We photographed Jonah's Froebel block towers. We delighted in Benji's habit of hiding the Cheerios box in the bathroom cabinet. He joined me in adopting the children's pronunciation mistakes, calling strawberries "strawbularries" and spooky "smooky."

Even with the intensity of love for my children, I felt something missing. Perhaps it was God. I grew up without: religion, a consistent home, clothes that fit, curtains, safety. I did not come from a family where I was adored. In the few photos from my childhood, my hair is unkempt, my smile crooked, my handed-down clothes worn thin and unfashionable.

I looked for God, hoping that a closer relationship with Him would allow me to feel safer in the world. Like Goldilocks, I kept trying different religions. The Unitarians were too agnostic. Unity bored me. The local Religious Science minister encouraged parishioners to pray for a Mercedes Benz as evidence of God's favor. People at Temple felt standoffish. Davening at the Sufi service felt weird. Finally, I found Vedanta. Their services, composed of meditation, lecture, and song, were both serious and joyful and ended with prasad, a social snack time. Vedanta taught a blend of Hinduism and Christianity. Here was their one central tenet: we were to lovingly offer our devotion to God.

And I experienced—if not a fall-on-your-knees miracle—something like a miracle's step- sister. Before the twins, I was a smoker. For twelve years I struggled with this habit. Quit ten times, once even for a whole year, then always returned to it. A moment of high stress, a day of boredom would morph into a pack of Marlboros and a morning hack. While taking a meditation and yoga intensive at Vedanta, everything changed. During a meditation focused on the third eye, a green light opened in my chest. I effortlessly quit smoking. I haven't craved a cigarette since.

As I grew more involved with the church, the wife of the lead minister told me about a crushing financial obligation they struggled to meet while raising funds to build the new Mandir. The debt stemmed from a lawsuit.

She explained, "Some years back, a church member in California had an affair with a married minister. When it came out, the minister wanted to stay with his wife. The woman was asked to move to another community the church operated. She agreed, but then filed a lawsuit. She alleged the founder also had an affair with her. The woman was unstable."

The people around me seemed so peaceful, so filled with love for God, the church so uniquely in-line with my hard-to-match religious prerequisites (feminist, pro-gay, not scientifically antagonistic, open to multiple paths to God), that I believed her. I believed her so much that I felt sorry for the small church trying to carry all this overhead. I could barely pay the electric bill, but donated every dollar I could spare.

After the twins turned two, I became more involved and began volunteering, tithing, and taking classes in addition to attending Sunday services. Felt closer to God than ever before. My husband complained and I ignored him. After all, he complained about the economy, our neighbor's neglected yard, our friend's furniture choices, the tax taken out of his unemployment check, bad lighting, stale coffee. Complaining was his hobby.

So what if my free time was spent doing volunteer work? It was all God's time anyway, all God's money. If I found myself twelve feet up in the air on a creaky scissor lift, painting the dome of the new mandir in spite (or maybe because) of my terror of falling, well that was God's will. God wanted me to grow spiritually, not be emotionally comfortable. I was down with that.

I met Swami K., the founder and leader, only once. He came from India to bless the new Mandir. During the service, Swami read from a newly church-published book he had written, an eight-hundred-page, seventy-five-dollar tome in which he recycled anecdotes and stories from previous books and meandered. I felt bad for judging. Who was I? I needed God's help with my arrogance and judgement.

After the service, a number of us stood outside on the steps. Swami K. walked toward me. For just a moment, his gaze felt cold, lizard-like and I squelched an urge to flee. We made small talk. He seemed bored but kept standing there. I made an excuse to leave and chalked up my discomfort to the fact that sometimes strangers freak me out, as well as intimidation in the presence of a holy man.

Around that time, I was switching jobs from non-profit social work to becoming a private practice therapist. On Wednesdays I worked for Sandy, a therapist with a busy business. Sandy belonged to a professional group of conservative Christian therapists who served predominantly Christian clients.

"I googled your name," she told me one day. "Your donations to that Vedanta church come up as public record. They run a bookstore owned by an untreated sex addict. It makes you look bad." Sandy was exactly the kind of person who would google a contract employee and follow their charitable donation history. I fought the urge to tell her to get a life. I changed the subject, feeling sorry for her.

I didn't ask, "What's your source of this information?" It took me a couple days before I even thought, "What if she knows something I don't?"

But finally, her story troubled me. Four hours of internet research later, I felt as if a bowling ball had been flung into my belly. Reading court testimony, websites from former members, news coverage of the trial and personal accounts revealed:

1. The founder, supposedly celibate, had a pattern of getting young female followers to perform fellatio on him.
2. It was six women, not just one, who testified in court to this fact.
3. The administration kept him in power and continued to call him "Swami," a specific religious title for celibates.
4. The church leaders decided that all these women who testified in court lied.
5. Because the church administration denied sexual exploitation occurred, there was no internal investigation, no response to prevent it from happening again, so no protection of their members.

I provided financial support to an organization that abused their members. I wanted to rewind and take back the years and hours and dollars I gave to these people. I had to leave the church. I wanted to vomit.

As a therapist specializing in PTSD, I can confidently state if six women came forward, that means many other women were exploited as well, but did not say anything due to embarrassment, shame, self-blame, and the realistic fear of being called sluts or liars.

For weeks afterward, I woke with an ache in my chest and didn't know why. Then I would remember: I left the church that I loved. Then more pain, more soul searching. I had to examine my own complicity, my own complacency. My willingness to look away, to not see.

When I first heard about the lawsuit, I asked questions. But instead of doing my own research, I gave others the job of informing me. And worse, I gave this job to the church administration, the very people who had a vested interest in making their leader innocent by discounting the whole thing.

My blanket trust was woven from passivity, a willingness to take things at face value because it got me off the hook.

Then there was my marriage. My husband got fired from every job, forgot to pay bills, come home on time, do what he agreed to do. He consistently demonstrated I couldn't count on him. Instead of facing reality, I tried to fix things by taking over more and more tasks. Earn the money. Pay the bills. Take care of the kids. Mow the grass. I kept looking for different, better help for him. The right diagnosis, the latest medication, a brain repatterning program, a better therapist, a job coach, a highly recommended couple's therapist. More social contact. Eventually I started hoping that one of us would die, and it didn't matter to me which one of us did.

Divorce is a heavy decision. I was afraid of everything: of hurting the kids, and of being too weak to make it on my own. Divorce meant losing time with the boys, and I didn't want to miss even one evening with my children. Benji was learning to lie to Jonah, which was both troubling and hilarious.

"Jonah it's spicy! And it's dirty!" He would say, emphasizing his words with sign language if he was eating something tasty that he didn't want to share. Jonah trusted Benji to be the brave one, to try new foods first and he trusted Benji's report. Like me with the church, Jonah didn't want to do his own investigation. He didn't believe me when I told him Benji was lying.

In the end, I divorced the church first and then left my marriage. And they were both the right, hard decisions. It has been ten years since my divorce and twelve since I left the church. I am happily remarried to a reliable man who works hard and makes me laugh. My children are in college, focused on chemistry and calculous classes and learning exactly how much pot they can smoke and still get good grades. Jonah no longer relies on Benji to try things first. I never found another church.

At some point, long after the children's story ends, Goldilocks grows up and stops eating other people's porridge. She learns to make her own. I am in that part of the story, in my own kitchen. Cooking is not as easy as eating what someone else makes. But it's my job to feed myself. It always was and it always will be. For finally figuring this out, I give thanks to God. For finding the courage to end my marriage and leave my church, I give thanks as well. It took me a while because I'm a slow learner, but at long last I've become a decent cook.

Waffle Cones
mark rosenblum

Jack Kellogg tapped the brake of his 1968 Dodge Dart as he backed out of the driveway. His hairline had surrendered to age, but his peripheral vision was sharp and he caught sight of his wife, Helen, racing out their front door waving a dish towel.

"Jack honey, did you remember the papers?"

"Of course," said Jack, patting a manila folder on the passenger seat.

"Oh, that's good. And honey—"

Here we go, thought Jack.

"—after you make copies, could you pick up some Rocky Road ice cream and those little waffle cones?"

Jack glanced at his watch. "Helen, I just want to make copies. Game starts at two and I don't want to miss it."

Her smile faded.

"Damn," whispered Jack. "Okay, I'll pick up the ice cream. But that overpriced, high-falutin' store with the waffle cones is in the opposite direction."

"Just the ice cream is fine, dear." She leaned into the car, kissed his cheek.

After countless tours of the parking lot surrounding Friend's Market, Jack finally found a space. He turned off the ignition, silencing Tony Bennett mid-croon. Jack wedged the folder under his arm and headed toward the market. A banner declared, 'Remodeling-Pardon Our Dust'.

After depositing an ungodly amount of dimes into a dusty copy machine in a forgotten rear corner of the store, he glanced at his watch. Fifteen minutes until the series final. He piled the copies into his folder and was headed back to the front of the store to leave when it hit him—pick up the Rocky Road.

He grabbed a basket. He searched the aisle signs, but most of them had been removed due to the remodel. He spotted a stock boy stacking cans.

"Where's the ice cream?"

No response.

Jack noticed wires dangling from his ears. He tapped his shoulder.

The boy removed his earphones—loud singing—definitely not Tony

Bennett.

"Yes sir?"

"Where's the ice cream?"

"Aisle nine, all new freezers."

Jack swung open the freezer door and the iciness immediately enveloped him. It was guard duty in Korea all over again. The North's offensive along with a five-day freeze kept his platoon hunkered down, and then the rains came. He felt a twitch in the fingers of his right hand, fingers frostbite almost robbed him of had it not been for the pretty, young M*A*S*H unit nurse who understood hypothermia better than the platoon medic.

"Glad you found the ice cream, sir," remarked the stock boy who startled Jack back into the present.

Jack made a hasty escape from the freezer section and headed to the registers.

All the lines were endless, so Jack chose one at random with hope the cashier would be swift. He strained to look past those ahead of him. The cashier was a girl in her late teens. Jack could barely see her face. Not just because of long hair dangling over her eyes, but because she never looked up, every movement a listless gesture. Each customer greeted with a robotic, "Hello," as they laid down items. She waved each purchase over the screen embedded in the counter; beeps acknowledged that the supermarket gods had accepted the offerings, steps repeated in dreary repetition.

Of all the cashier lanes, thought Jack, he picked the one operated by a Zombie.

Jack was now close enough to notice the clerk's ring—a silver skull with onyx eyes—a fitting piece of jewelry for the undead.

He scrutinized those ahead of him. There was Coupon Clipper, an elderly woman purchasing endless cans of cat food; Yelling Mother, a woman demanding her young daughter stop picking up impulse items; and finally, Fatigue Guy, a tall young man in army fatigues.

Jack was about to take another habitual glance at his watch when an uneasy feeling made him take greater notice of Fatigue Guy. He wasn't carrying any items. He kept his head low, a cap angled downward just above his eyes, eyes that observed Zombie Cashier without blinking. The young man's right hand was in a cast, his left hand in his pocket.

Jack now began to seriously consider if Fatigue Guy might be going to rob the joint. Crazy Guy Shoots Up Market—that's what the headline will read—with the sub-headline, Veteran Ironically Killed Prior to Filing New Medicare Death Benefit Forms.

Coupon Clipper was gone. Yelling Mother finished her transaction, and Zombie Cashier did not look up, she just mumbled "Hello" to Fatigue Guy.

"Marlboros please."

She placed the pack over the scanner. Beep. Fatigue Guy removed his left hand from his pocket. No gun.

Fatigue Guy cupped his hand directly over Zombie Cashier's while she held the cigarettes. Jack noticed his ring, identical to the clerk's. Zombie Cashier looked up at Fatigue Guy and abruptly covered her mouth to silence a squeal. She then began to sob.

"Minor wound from Iraqi forces . . . early discharge . . . wanted to surprise you . . . I love you." Words blended between kisses across the counter.

Fatigue Guy said they would meet tonight. A last kiss. He departed. She wiped away tears with the sleeve of her smock and quickly ran fingers through her hair, brushing it behind her ears. She made eye contact with Jack and smiled.

"Hello sir, sorry for the delay."

Helen held the door open as Jack carried in the groceries, his car keys, and the folder.

"I was beginning to worry," said Helen.

"Remodeling the market, renovating everything except the parking lot."

"Oh, my," she said as she relieved him of the shopping bag and folder and vanished into the kitchen.

Jack tossed his keys into a bowl resting on a table at the end of the hallway. The bowl, lacquered wood with carved Korean symbols sat between two framed photos. One depicted a young Jack—army helmet askew upon his head, cocky grin across his face, rifle held steadfast at his side. The other photo, the one Jack lingered over before turning on the game, depicted a young Helen—head peering out the flap of a snow-covered tent, locks of curly hair and a reassuring smile worn as proudly as her M*A*S*H unit's nurse's uniform.

In the kitchen, Helen removed the ice cream from the Friend's Market bag. She reached in again to remove a second item, this one in a smaller bag emblazoned with the name of a different store. She smiled as she held her little waffle cones.

King City
matthew j. andrews

I remember it as freedom, as aimless roaming under cloudy skies, as open doors up and down the block, as spades in the dirt and every sharp rock an arrowhead, as kickball in the street and baseball in empty lots, as junkyard sculptures, as snacks shoved hurriedly into backpacks, as forts in half-finished homes, as mountain horizons inching closer to our expanding reach.

My parents scoff at the memory: *we were so miserable, so poor, so alone, and you were the only kid who didn't speak Spanish.*

An Honest Man

amanda ice

I read once that stairways used to be built unevenly. It was a way to throw off intruders in medieval times. Some steps taller, some shorter. Some diagonal. When's the last time anyone today had to consciously think about each step walking up or down stairs? There are regulations about these things now. People take great care to provide a swift stair-walking experience.

I imagine walking up these medieval staircases wasn't too bad. Might trip and scrape a knee. Don't carry anything of value. Downstairs would have been the scary part. Someone might leave with scabs on their palms and shins or split their head open. Maybe even bump down each step face down, skin sliding off until their face is lumpy carnage at the bottom, and people must have been like, oh no, another stair accident. As frequent and tragic as fender-benders.

This is what I think about as I walk up these stairs to your apartment.

You're wrapped in a pink towel when you open the door, your hair dripping down your arm, off your elbow onto your carpet. I always thought it was sort of gross that you don't mind things like soggy carpet.

You ask me, "Do you want some cake? Yesterday was my birthday. I have leftover cake."

"No thanks," I say, and make my way to sit at your table.

"Why not? Please have some, there's half of it left and I live alone. I don't want to eat it all."

You haven't cleaned since your party last night. Empty beer cans are still sprinkled around.

You disappear into your bedroom for a minute and come back out with a big t-shirt over your little shorts. There's a wet spot on your shoulder where most of your hair rests. You stop and look at me. "Why are you sitting at the table? Go sit on the couch. You're being too formal."

"I don't want to get comfortable," I tell you.

"If you're going to sit at the table, at least eat some cake."

"I won't be here long." This is me being sensible. Efficient. Not wasting time.

You walk to the fridge and take out the cake. What's left over is a semi-circle. It's white cake covered in white frosting with bulbous, sugary balloons in primary colors like you've just turned twenty years younger than you are.

"Mia, I don't want cake," I tell you.

You pick up the cake cutter from the sink and start washing it. "Don't call me that," you say, "Just call me Babe, or Honey or something. You're still acting too formal. Relax!" You smile to yourself, and I start to feel bad.

The thought of tasting frosting so thick with sweetness while this tiny worm of guilt crawls in my stomach makes me feel nauseous.

"No, Mia, I'm trying to break up with you."

You pause for a few seconds, then take out a plate.

"I really don't want any. I'm not staying long."

"You didn't think you would be staying long?" You say this as you slice a big piece, almost half of what is there. "You thought you could just tell me that and leave? Just in and out like that?"

"You know I really like you. I have a lot of fun with you, but—"

"No no no." You wave the cake cutter around as you speak. "You've just started and that's the most inauthentic thing I've heard in my entire life. Don't patronize me. I don't want to hear the bland, stock phrase speech you've come up with. I want to know why."

I don't want to tell you. I'm half guilty and half afraid; there's no room for cake in me, but you place it before me anyway. The plate lands with a clank on the table.

I don't want to tell you about the other girl. I don't want to tell you I've been sleeping at her place the past three nights. I don't want to tell you that we met at your least favorite bar, or that her teeth are straighter than yours, or that she doesn't leave wet towels on the floor, or that she wouldn't force feed me cake, but these are the only things occupying my mind.

You're still waiting for my answer, eyes wild like a kitten learning to pounce, holding the cake cutter in the air.

"I've been cheating on you," I say. This is me being responsible, being an honest man. I'm cleaning up my mess. Putting things in order.

"I thought you were here to apologize for forgetting my birthday yesterday. I thought you were going to give me a present or something. You didn't even bring me a gift."

"I don't know, I thought that might make it worse. You don't want to be patronized, but you expect a gift when I break up with you." A consolation prize. A spirit award. A trophy engraved, *sorry I found someone else, better luck next time.*

"Just eat the stupid cake already!" You're screaming now, and I'm wondering what your neighbors are thinking.

I remember their knocks on the wall when we laughed too hard at the warped animals and faces we made on your popcorn ceiling. Or our spontaneous YouTube karaoke nights. Or their knocking when you wailed in front of the mirror naked, socking yourself in the stomach.

I remember your skinny friend you tried to force feed nearly a whole bottle of whiskey the last time we went out. You said you didn't want to get too drunk, lived vicariously through her vomit and slurred words. You left her sloppy and slow at the party.

I imagine your mother force feeding you. Giving you spoonful after spoonful until you had all this fat you had to purge when you moved out. You gagged and puked all throughout college. Now you post long paragraphs about struggle and mental health with every push-up bra selfie.

I know you're the one who wants to eat the cake.

I notice you forgot to get me a fork.

"I'm not a bad person," I say, speaking from the heart now. "I've been trying to figure out why I did it. I think maybe it's because my mom would always cheat on my dad."

"I met your parents. They're happily married." You're speaking at the same volume as your scream, but with less harshness in your throat.

"I know. It's still a secret. She doesn't know I know. But she's always talking to this person named Leslie, and that *could* be a man's name…"

You laugh. You're not paying attention to me. "Why do this a week after introducing me to them? What was the point?"

I try not to let your narcissism annoy me this time. This is me being patient. Understanding. Gently, I continue, "Or maybe it's because this girl I was with in high school cheated on me once, well, practically cheated on me. She had a crush on her science teacher."

"I actually liked you, Jasper." You say my name like a curse word, like you have to spit it out of your mouth. "I kept making excuses for you when my friends asked why you weren't at my birthday party last night. I told them you were probably sick, or you must have run into an emergency."

"I think maybe that girl impacted me more than I thought. You see, I didn't acknowledge the trauma it caused me at the time, and maybe this was just my way of releasing it."

You're still not acknowledging me. Instead, you say, "You could have at least responded to my texts last night. I was *worried* about you."

Three knocks on the wall across from us. Your neighbor. You throw the cake cutter at them. A smear of red frosting stays there.

I take that as my cue to leave.

"The least you can do," you pick up the plate and follow me out the door, "after cheating on me, is eat the freaking cake."

If there's one thing I've learned about you in this experience, it's that you are not immune to throwing things, so I quicken my pace down the stairs.

I've always walked faster than you, but I don't expect myself to be so far ahead when you call me. I only turn around because your voice has lost its edge and sounds more desperate. More child-like. Sad.

It would have made more sense if you were wearing heels or something, but you were still barefoot. Maybe if someone had spilled something beforehand, or if you had a history of these things. But you're perfectly coordinated.

Even on these immaculately calculated, levelled steps, equipped with railings on both sides. Even though you must have walked these steps a hundred times before.

In your whirl of rage, you were too eager and missed a step. The plate went flying above you like a frisbee and the cake slid off it, coloring a couple steps red, blue, yellow and white. The porcelain clamored somewhere like a rushed windchime. Before sliding down, you tried to plant your feet to stop yourself but your momentum pushed you forward, face first. Your chin landed with a thump on the corner of a step. The blood burst out of your face like fireworks. Blood landing on frosting landing on stairs, in your hair and on your clothes. I thought that was all from your split chin until I saw a little pink blob land by my feet. Half of your tongue.

The rest of you was still skidding down the stairs, your chin bobbing against each of them, smearing blood across white cake across the steps across your arms and shirt.

I realized I forgot to say I was sorry.

Boeing Wonderland

heather bourbeau

Years before Levittown, Hollywood was called in
to sell American dream to Japanese pilots who never came.

Plywood and clapboard, chicken wire and burlap,
camouflage, feathers, and spun glass. Real grass and real weeds.

"Synthetic Street" and "Burlap Boulevard," wink and nod.
Houses too small, streets too quiet.

26 acres of fantasy above factory hid thousands of women,
thousands of men, thousands of new bombs.

Then infamy and fear exchanged roles. Victim became hunter.
Months after firebombing Tokyo, contract to dismantle the farce.

Weeks before Nagasaki and Hiroshima, publicity photos released.
Young white women in fitted suits or short skirts and bikini tops,

hair coifed—nary a uniform, hardly a man—enjoying ersatz
breaks, sunbathing, strolling, chatting where just before,

they could not go. Celebrating successful lies through more
deception. The great rehearsal for a suburban swell.

Formation—December 2016

rebecca beardsall

Auckland skyline rests behind me. Sky Tower points the way home. The tide snakes dark water into the mudflats of Henderson Creek, creating a divide.

Land holds our stories, the dust, the dirt, our DNA. This land memory.

On the floor, feeling Auckland on my back. Jet, our six-year-old grandson, carries a large white cardboard box out of his room. His still-growing arms struggle under the weight. Curious to see what is hidden inside, I watch him slide the box the rest of the way into the lounge on the grey carpet.

Grammie, come look at this. Grammie, they call me, although I've never had children of my own. I remain Rebecca to my stepson, Reece.

Inside, a kaleidoscope of gemstones, minerals, and rocks. He takes each treasure out and tells me its story. *This one I picked up when I was walking with Nana. And this one I got near the beach. Look, jasper. It has pretty brown lines.* When he notices he has more than one of the same kind, he hands a stone to me and says, *You can have this one.* I dutifully take the few he gives me and place them in a circle in front of my crossed legs.

Many in Jet's collection come from gem stores–polished amethyst, sliced agates, spires of crystal–but hidden amongst the purchased are the found. We might not share blood, but we are both collectors. My house is filled with jars, dishes, pottery chalices holding my secrets. Stones, shells, twigs, seeds from my travels.

I pick up an almost translucent stone with lines of blue-green veins. It looks like algae swaying in the tide, frozen in the briefest of moments. I ask about the type of stone and where he found it. He holds it in his hands, twisting it around just as I did, *I'm not sure, but you can have it.*

I don't want to take it, Jet. I just thought it was pretty.

I never found out the story of how this little stone found its way into Jet's collection, but it now has a story. Our story. Jet and me sitting in the lounge in Massey as we talk about collecting natural, earth-made prizes.

In each piece we touch, we hear the story and add our moment to the littlest piece of mineral. Jet gives me a small piece of quartz crystal, the size of my pinky toe. He tells me that I need to squeeze real hard when I am sick or scared, because it will make me feel better. He hefts a larger piece of quartz crystal and demonstrates for me, *This is the one I hold on to when I'm sick. Real tight, like this. See?*

What's this? I raise up a golden blob. It feels much lighter than a stone. *Oh, that's kauri gum. I have a big one here.* He pulls out a piece the size of his fist.

Really? I have never held kauri gum before. I remember my husband telling me kauri gum is fossilized sap of the kauri tree. As the trees grow, they shed their bark, and the gum adhering to the bark sloughs off. It starts to harden and through time it fossilizes.

Māori used kauri gum for generations – for chewing gum, for starting fires, for tattooing – before the Pākehā arrived. However, the kauri gum industry started around 1814 when settlers sent a shipment back to London. The kauri gum shipment supposedly ended up in the Thames, but that first shipment was the start of a Northland industry.

Rolling the kauri gum in my palm. The gum, a resin created by the kauri to protect itself, now hardened, rests in my hand. What's its story? What tree did it come from? Who dug it up? Why is it here in Jet's box of earthly minerals?

I hold the kauri gum for a few more minutes, rubbing my fingers on the glossy edges where it broke off from a larger piece before I place it gingerly back on the floor.

As we clean up the multitudes of orbs, I gather the few Jet selected for me and start to place them back in the box.

No, Grammie, those are yours. One collector to another, I accept the gifts. I gather them into a Ziploc bag and add a few more from our trip around New Zealand. Packing our bags to leave Auckland, Jet asks me if I still have my gems. I nod.

The stones Jet gave me sit next to my computer in a little green bowl that used to belong to my paternal grandmother, Grammy Helm. In the bowl amongst the shells and stones a golden nugget of kauri gum rests to remind me that land, even its piece, has memory. A story stored inside.

We collectors of treasures are also collectors of stories. Following the call to gather up a rock, a pebble, a shell. Each stone in my green bowl holds Jet's story and my memory inside of it. Such large work for something so small.

Issue 11 Contributors

Matthew J. Andrews is a private investigator and writer whose poetry has appeared or is forthcoming in *Orange Blossom Review*, *Funicular Magazine*, and *EcoTheo Review*, among others. His debut chapbook, *I Close My Eyes* and *I Almost Remember*, is forthcoming from Finishing Line Press. He can be contacted at matthewjandrews.com.

L. L. Babb has been a teacher at the Writers Studio San Francisco and on-line since 2008. Her work has appeared or is forthcoming in *Cleaver Magazine*, *West Marin Review*, *The MacGuffin*, *Green Hills Literary Lantern*, *Signal Mountain Review*, and elsewhere. She was voted first in the fiction category for *Sixfold Magazine's* winter 2018 issue and was a finalist in the 2016 Epiphany Spring Fiction Contest.

Rebecca Beardsall (MA, Lehigh University; MFA, Western Washington University) is the author of *My Place in the Spiral*. Rebecca is the prose editor at *Psaltery & Lyre* and the nonfiction editor at *Minerva Rising*. Her poetry and essays have appeared in *Thimble*, *SWIMM*, *West Texas Review*, *Two Cities Review*, *Poetry NZ*, and *Rag Queen Periodical*. She wrote and co-edited three books, including *Philadelphia Reflections: Stories from the Delaware to the Schuylkill*. Find her at: rebeccabeardsall.com

Heather Bourbeau's work has appeared in 100 Word Story, *Alaska Quarterly Review*, *The Kenyon Review*, *Meridian*, *The Stockholm Review of Literature*, and SWWIM. She has worked with various UN agencies, including the UN peacekeeping mission in Liberia and UNICEF Somalia. Her recently completed collection "Monarch" is a poetic memoir of overlooked histories from the American West she was raised in.

C.P. Bruno studied English under James P. Degnan at Santa Clara University.

Allisa Cherry was born and raised in a rural community in the southwest of the United States. She has since relocated to Portland, OR where she works as a writing tutor and small-scale urban farmer and has recently completed an MFA in poetry at Pacific University. Her work has received

Pushcart Prize nominations from *San Pedro River Review* and *High Desert Journal*, and can be read in *Westchester Review* and *Tar River Poetry*.

T. Clear, Seattle poet, has been writing and publishing her work since the late 1970's. Recent publications include *terrain.org, The American Journal of Poetry* and *South Florida Poetry Journal*. Her book, "A House, Undone," is forthcoming from MoonPath press in 2022. Pending pandemic cancellations, join her at Poets at Carrowholly in September, 2022, in the west of Ireland. She can be found at tclearpoet.com.

James Giffin is a multimedia consultant and emerging writer living in San Diego. An alumnus of San Francisco State University, he currently sits as the Design Editor and Creative Nonfiction Editor of *Fourteen Hills*. His work has also appeared in *Heartwood Literary Magazine*.

Jamie A. Grove's work has been featured in *Black Fox Literary*, *805 Lit+Art*, and *Parentheses Journal*, among others. She has been nominated for the Best of the Net and has work forthcoming in 2021 from Subjectiv. and Propertius Press. She lives on the dry side of Oregon with her family, where she reads when she should be writing and writes when she wishes she was reading.

Nancy Hill is a writer/photographer/photojournalist living in Oregon. Her work has been published in regional and national publications as well as literary journals, both in print and online. Her photographic work has appeared in galleries and in print. Now that her two sons are grown, her household has shrunk to just her and her collie, Frankenstein.

Amanda Ice is an emerging poet and fiction writer freshly graduated with an English degree from CSULB. Her poetry has been selected to appear in Riprap and Sonder Midwest.

Seth Jani lives in Seattle, WA and is the founder of Seven CirclePress (www.sevencirclepress.com). Their work has appeared in *The American Poetry Journal, Chiron Review, Ghost City Review, Rust+Moth* and *Pretty Owl Poetry*, among others. Their full-length collection, *Night Fable*, was published by FutureCycle Press in 2018. Visit them at www.sethjani.com.

Jennifer Kim grew up under the searing sun of Northern California, in a home that featured a cherry tree blooming before it. She studied Philosophy and Politics at Pomona College, then law at the University of Pennsylvania, before returning home to California where her beloved family and childhood collection of books reside. Jennifer has previously published "Transcendental Self" in Brown's *Journal of Philosophy, Politics, and Economics*, and she writes in frequently to Friday Flash Fiction.

Linda Malnack is the author of two poetry chapbooks, *21 Boxes* (dancing girl press) and *Bone Beads* (Paper Boat Press). Her poetry appears in *Prairie Schooner, the Seattle Review, Amherst Review, Southern Humanities Review, Blackbird*, and elsewhere. Linda is an Assistant Poetry Editor for *Crab Creek Review*.

Caitlin Mitchel-Markley, formerly an attorney, is a neurodivergent poet and stay-at-home mom to three incredible children. She now enjoys spending her time writing poetry, cuddling her lovely husband, and sharing her love of all things geeky with her amazing kids. Her work has recently appeared or is forthcoming in *Crosswinds Poetry Journal, La Piccioletta Barca*, the second volume of *Aurora: The Allegory Ridge Poetry Anthology*, and elsewhere.

Nellie Papsdorf is a writer and social worker from Portland, Oregon. Her poetry has been published or is forthcoming in *SUSAN / The Journal, HASH Journal*, and *Witch Craft Magazine*, among others. You can find her on Instagram @worldsbiggestballofyarn.

Morgan Reed has worked in industry in the Midwest, education at the Sorbonne, and multimedia consulting and fine art painting in California. With a lifelong interest in foreign cultures, he has also done research and translation in many languages. Poetry has been part of his life since childhood: he recently returned to writing it.

Mark Rosenblum is a New York native who now lives in Southern California where he misses the taste of real pizza and good deli food. He attempts not to drive his wife crazy but tends to fail miserably. His eclectic ramblings of fiction and poetry appear in *Monkeybicycle, Penduline, Vine Leaves, the Raleigh Review, Flash Frontier* and other journals.

Tanya Ruckstuhl is a clinical social worker in Seattle specializing in anxiety disorders and mother or stepmother to three nineteen-year-olds who crown her biggest dork on the planet. She loves hanging out in her garden and befriending people with vastly different political belief systems. She writes an award-winning mental health blog, https://seattletherapist. wordpress.com/ and is working on an environmental thriller.

Nina Schuyler is the author of the award-winning novel, *The Translator*, and the bestseller, *How to Write Stunning Sentences*. She teaches creative writing at the University of San Francisco. and The Writing Room.

Joanell Serra is a poet, playwright, novelist and essayist from Northern California, with work published in *Eclectica, Blue Lake Review, Black Fox Literary Magazine, Manifest-station, Poydras Review* and elsewhere. Books include *The Vines We Planted* (Wido, 2018) and *(Her)oics Anthology*, a collection of women's essays about the pandemic (Regal House Publishing, 2021). Her work has won multiple writing contests

DeAnna Tibbs is a mother, photographer, and writer from Oakland, CA. She spends her free time attempting to brush her three unfriendly cats and grow a tomato that isn't mealy. This is the first publication of her writing. Her photography has been included in *Molecule–a tiny lit mag, When Pens Bloom: A Chapbook Collaboration*, and publications of the East Bay Regional Park District, as well as local galleries. You can find DeAnna under the redwoods or on Instagram @deannadtibbs

Heather Whited is a teacher and writer who lives in Portland, Oregon. Her work has appeared in several literary magazines.